Teleos The Gold City

D.L. Miller

Keep on keeping on publishing company LLC

About Author

D.L. Miller Is a believer in Jesus Christ. He came to know Christ when he was 28 years old. A stutter by birth. He has faced many challenges over the years. He still questions why God gave him this gift that he thinks is a curse. Over the years, he has learned to accept his stutter as himself. Still battling self-worth and doubt. He has stepped out of his comfort zone and following his dream. By taking story from the Old and New testament and turn them into a fiction adventure. With the hope of bring young and old readers to the stories of the bible. As he reads the word of God. His imagination runs wild on the stories that God tells. He like to fill in the blanks. That's how he came up with the story Teleos the Gold City. The story of Adam and Eve inspired it (Genesis 3).

Contents

Chapter 1: And There Was Darkness

In the beginning, Theodore created a great civilization. A perfect world, some would say. Greater than any other place on earth. It was time for Theodore to start a new civilization on earth. He sent a team of surveyors out to search for a place that a greater civilization could be built. They went into a part of earth that has never been explored before. A place where the sun has never shined before. A place of total darkness. People called this part of earth the dark side. Everyone has been afraid of this area. This was all some strange phenomenon, something that they had just had no chance of knowing before; back in the city from which they had come from. There had been no such thing as darkness, not even a little. Regardless of the time of the day, the city had always been illuminated, with an encased bright light that never could go dim.

The team of surveyors came back 28 days later and reported back to Theodore. They gave him their report on the land. It had a spring of water that branched out into 4 rivers. The only issue was the darkness. Theodore loved a challenge. He was a visionary; forward thinker; non-traditional list and a man of wisdom. Some would say he was a god for his physical size and strength, his mind was powerful and whatever he thought of, he made sure it came to life through determination and knowledge, inspiring those close to trust in him. This same energy he gives to the men working with him, to a great extent.Theodore went out to see this glorious land for himself. It amazed him how big it was and the spring that turned into 4 rivers was marvelous. He said to himself, this is a place where milk and honey will flow throughout eternity. Meaning it was rich in all minerals and natural resources but one. "Light."Where Theodore now stood. The darkness was deep and thick, unheard of back in the former city, but it did not discourage Theodore or put him off in this new environment. Instead, he saw the blackness as an opportunity, one that could be good. In fact, he was ready to make it exactly that.

The question was, where would they get light from? There had to be an energy source that could produce light.Theodore sent out his trusted mineralogist to search north of the spring to find an energy source to produce light for this great city.They set off to explore. After 200 kilometers, their mineral meter made an alarming sound. Alerting that mineral was below their feet. They started digging and found this Anonymous quartz crystal. They gathered their team of engineers to remove the quartz crystal. As they rigged up the cables and pulleys to lift the quartz out of the ground, one cable broke, causing the crystal to come out of the rigging and falling to the ground. When the crystal hit the ground, it felt like a great earthquake. The ground shook so much, causing the crystal to crack and the vibration inside the crystal that omitted a glorious light that lit up the whole dark side of the earth. Now, having a light source that would never end, they could start building the city.

Even though this was an enormous task, Theodore knew before-hand that it would take all his charisma and more to motivate his men to accomplish what he knew would be a far more appealing life for all.

They arrived there in droves and with keenness, zeal flowing from them, eager to get on with the task ahead, each one clamoring to impress the great Theodore with their mighty work ethic!

Then they cast their gazes around. "So, Theodore. Where shall we build?" they asked one after the other. "Lead us to the chosen place. There, we can make a start." Where the 4 rivers start. "We will build as the rivers flow." The spring will be the center of the city and we will go beyond the Crystal. This *great* city will be called Teleos.

After their arrival, some of these men lost hope before they had even begun, taking in the sheer scale of the daunting task Theodore had laid out before them.

But few dared question Theodore's plans and determination.

The majority soon brought into line those who did and their greater resolve.

Each man remained keen to show how well he could carry out his master's commands. In fact, a few judged it might even be a test to see who would attempt it and who would refuse, like a stubborn goat refusing to move along a green pathway to find the drinking water.

This task was on another level, humongous beyond anything to which they had been subjected before, testing even the most resilient of Theodore's workers.

But the few who dared voice such a theory received scorn from every side. They learned to shut their mouths and join in the fervor, proclaiming, "Oh! What an amazing land to build on!"

Even if they doubted, they would have to doubt silently. Most understood Theodore's outlook and what he hoped to achieve, but there was always that burning question: did he even know that this feat was possible? *Was* it? And even if it were to be possible, then at what cost and would that cost be worth it in the end? One thing they all knew and agreed on was that many would suffer along the way, both physically and mentally, due to the relentless workload and pressure of achieving Theodore's goals. They trudged on in resolute silence, having no alternative.

They always reminded themselves of one thing:

"Let us remember Theodore is our most visionary, prominent leader," they muttered among themselves. Whatever Theodore said, that was what had to happen. Progress could not be reached in this godforsaken place otherwise. It was all down to them and their mind-set.

They would build, and they built.

Even having a hierarchical structure in place, the people said Theodore was no fool, constantly overseeing the progression of his dream, supporting especially those at the very bottom and offering encouragement where he saw it was necessary.

Theodore was feeding them energy through hope, reviving their strength daily, one of the many reasons he'd gained so much respect from each one of his followers. In short, Theodore was a living legend who could pick up the bleakest scenario and revive it.

Theodore's plan—and all agreed it was mighty—creating the most spectacular city. The initial phase involved the preparation of the land, something that in itself took far longer than expected, days rolling into weeks before those loyal to Theodore could even start building his city of dreams.

As expected, the relentless workload claimed many lives from day one.

Some losses were through pure exhaustion, others were just accidental deaths caused by fatigue, stupid decisions and rash moves on dangerous terrain. Morale would dip. Often, the morale and enthusiasm among the workers would drop so low that Theodore would gather in his trusted men, delivering a speech so captivating that it would soon motivate them to continue.

It took days, weeks, months, and in the end,it took a few years for the city to look just like Theodore envisioned. For no one denied, Theodore *was* a man of vision.

That old familiar cry would reach their lips again as they chanted:

"Hail Theodore, our visionary master!"

Some were aspiring to become versions of Theodore, men to look up to.

They brought their sons from young ages to learn from Theodore, their renowned leader, hoping they too would absorb the teachings of this great man himself.

The sons grew and bore their own sons, then their own sons again in turn, and the city grew in numbers and fame, each passing through the same teachings inspired by the great man Theodore.

Many neighboring cities, and even those farther afield, came to form an alliance with Theodore and his city, Teleos.

Anyone could see his power from afar, knowing better than to be enemies with him.

And eventually, the city covered the whole side of the earth that was once called the dark side of the earth.

L ife was beautiful at Teleos.

Perfect.

Well, it would be, wouldn't it? Because they still had their *progressive man* at their helm!

Milk and honey flowed through the entire land and there was peace as Theodore led with all the wisdom and power that he had. There was a sweet aroma in the air.

Far and wide, there was not one city that was like Teleos, not one that could claim to be this perfect on earth. However, something the populace did not know was that Theodore himself was dissatisfied. He was left not feeling very successful at times.

In fact, he still felt as though *he* was incomplete.

Something was still missing.

He pondered, realizing what he needed to complete his great work—his son. After all, most men in these times aspired to reach the unattainable for one reason only, and this was so they had something worthy to pass to their sons who would continue the work long after they passed on.

Theodore contacted his son Andrew and asked him to visit the new city.

"Master!" Michael, Theodore's chief right-hand man, cried out, rushing into the vast room with a wad of parchment in hand. As he ran, he slipped and skidded on the highly polished marble tiles, then swung around the giant alabaster columns by putting out a hand to steady himself.

Michael was most loyal, having worked alongside Theodore faithfully when the city was still being built from the ground up. Michael had remained by Theodore's side, never faltering.

"Yes, Michael," Theodore answered, seated calmly by a dark wood writing desk in the far alcove, looking out of a giant arched open window onto the lush, dense greenery of date palms.

Under the tropical sun, a spectacular fountain recycled the same glittering water over and over in the center of the palms, creating a soothing sound to relax Theodore's always active mind.

Its restfulness was in contrast to Michael's frantic running about.

But Theodore was used to seeing Michael dashing around like a hurricane wherever he went.

"Master, it is Andrew. He requires an audience with you!" Michael exclaimed.

"Andrew? What did he say?"

"Well, nothing, Master. Nothing at all. Just that he needs to speak with you. That is all."

"And it is a matter of great urgency?"

"No, Master. Not that I know of," answered Michael.

Theodore's face broke into a grin. Well, of course, it wasn't urgent.

"Is he here or did he send word?"

"He is here, Master. He waits in the courtyard."

"Thank you, Michael. Then let us not wait. Please bring him through." Theodore smiled again. "He has come because I invited him here. Well, he was in the city already."

It was never clear why the good Michael always entered in such a tremendous hurry, almost killing himself to get there fast. It was enough to fray a man's nerves, even those of Theodore.

Yet there was never any urgency, was there?

This particular visit between father and son had been a week in its making.

Shortly after, the doors flung open, and Andrew strode in, much slower and calmer.

There was no doubting he was Theodore's progeny.

His shoulders were just as broad as his father's and when he spoke, his booming deep voice, like Theodore's, filled the room. It was only his first week living in Teleos, so he knew little about the city yet, but the people said he walked around confidently, asking many questions.

Many would stop in awe, looking at the unmistakable figure of Andrew, Theodore's son.

"Son! Oh, Son, it's so good to see you," Theodore said with a smile, so proud to see Andrew standing before him. "Please, do come here to your father."

"Father!" Andrew approached the man long since his living idol. "Father, how good to see you again! And in this marvel of a place, too! I feel as though I have woken in a dreamland."

Theodore stood, walking to greet his son with open arms. "Look at you, Son."

"Good day, Father," Andrew replied, accepting his father's open arms, heaving a deep sigh.

"You have come to see me at last? You have found time in your busy schedule?"

He was jesting; everyone knew Andrew was mostly a man of leisure these days, and that was why he was rarely seen in these parts or around his father—for they also knew that wherever their progressive leader Theodore was, plenty of hard manual labor would be on offer.

Andrew was never around for it, instead favoring burying his head in books.

"And to what do I owe this pleasure?" Theodore said. "You received my missive?"

"There are many things I want to know, Father. But yes, your letter intrigued me, so I came. You asked me to take a visit to Teleos, to look around and to give my impressions. Most importantly, I want to know everything about Teleos," Andrew said. "I have witnessed it with my own eyes, and I stand in awe of you. I want to know everything about this great city."

"It is my father's city, so I wish to know all about it. How you run it and how you control it."

"Ah! Yes, you do. You need to."

Andrew's face took on a bemused expression. He had said he wished to. Now, his father was asserting he *needed* to! Need? Why *need?*

"Then show me, Father! I want to know it all," Andrew said, his pale face reddening at the thought of some manual labor his father might expect of him. He continued showing interest, since it was the only way to behave in front of Theodore.

He had learned as much growing up. It was to Theodore's great disappointment when Andrew had proclaimed that his only wish in life was to study! To be an academic!

They'd had a disagreement about it before Theodore finally gave in, funding his study. There was never any sense in making a boy follow a course in which he was reluctant. He could only hope that Andrew would come around to bigger and better things someday. Such as now…

"I should like to know how it was built, and how long it took to build this splendid green oasis of a city out of the nothingness of the wasteland and ruins," said Andrew, still laying it on thick to impress his father. Theodore gave a skeptical look; he remained sure the boy had only agreed to come because he believed Teleos was finally complete and the hard work was all finished.

Though Andrew possessed his father's looks, it was widely known that his work ethic was sadly still a little lacking. It was unlikely Andrew would show up anywhere during a time of great effort to build anything. Once it was done, you could be sure he would arrive, stating an interest. Well, such as right now, and here he was. This time, Theodore had a plan for him.

Andrew clearly marveled at what his father had achieved, taking in the delightful room.

He remembered the whispers about his good father, words that left everyone's lips.

Theodore is a very progressive man. He makes sure we move forward! Theodore has hidden secrets, wonders beyond belief to aid in his progress everywhere he goes!

"And I will surely show you everything, Son. I have been watching you, Andrew," Theodore said after a stretch of silence. "And you really deserve to see the city, meet those closest to me, and to own it someday very soon. Though 'tis a pity you missed all the construction of it."

Andrew gaped. Was his father serious?

Inside, Theodore wore a wide smile, jesting with his son, poking fun at him.

Andrew undoubtedly understood his father's achievement. He also would have known how much Theodore was respected, not just by his own people here in Teleos, but also far beyond in the surrounding cities. Andrew seemed excited to be with his father in this great city with fantastic people, wanting to be involved in everything that happened around him.

He wished to take some of the glory upon himself, no doubt.

However, a man less cynical might say he wanted nothing more than to emulate his father, so there was no better way than to spend as much time with the great man as he possibly could.

It just took time to fire him up, and he needed to see a completed job before he grew excited.

"Yes, Father! Someday soon, in the next decade or two, I shall take over your role."

"Son, please come with me. We have so much to see, and you have so much to learn, but I have the greatest confidence in you. After all, you are my son, my only heir."

For now, he would give Andrew the benefit of doubt; he loved his son, after all. And he had never been a lazy boy once he got started on something. It was just that he was slow in starting.

Well, very slow—so slow as to be a non-starter at times. And Theodore, being so progressive himself as everyone said about him, knew exactly how to fix this trait in him!

Following closely behind his father, Andrew emulated Theodore's posture and movement, soft yet determined, much like his father's character. Theodore chose carefully where he would place his foot, and even if he moved with caution, he always got there in the end.

And that was how he also led, never giving up, never admitting the end or the goal might seem out of sight. He would just keep on moving forward, even if there were many steps back.

"One step at a time," he'd say. "If you continue with one foot forward, there is no way you shall not get there. And the same with a magnificent construction. You can say it is too difficult or you can carry on just quietly laying down a brick or a stone, one at a time, until it is done."

This was something Andrew would like to learn for himself—to be dogged and be sure.

There was no doubting Theodore was a formidable man, but he also had a level of compassion rarely found in someone with his power and fearsome reputation. It was a rare mix that certainly had helped him gain the trust and confidence of those around him and beyond.

Even after such a short time in his father's company, Andrew was coming to learn this too, studying his father in great detail—his mannerisms, his presence and the way he conducted himself in front of others. He wanted to mirror his father, even taking on board the smallest aspect of his character; he noted every minute detail and practiced it when he was in his room.

Theodore said little, keeping Andrew in suspense for what he intended to show his son first.

Following on, they reached a tall building shaped like a tower and after a twist of tall stone stairs in a sandy hue, arrived at the top, where a breeze was blowing, ruffling their hair.

"Well, what do you think?"

"Father, I don't know what to say! This is just...! Look, there are so many beautiful buildings in the city, Father!" Andrew cried out in excitement when he entered the room at the top of the tower. "It's so high, Father. I never envisaged this."

He looked through the window on top of the world. Then they ventured arm in arm through a wide opening onto a parapet overlooking everything. Andrew had just turned eighteen now, and this was as high a place as any he had ever visited in his young life. He marveled at the sight.

It was rare for a youth to get to stand on a parapet except for when he became a leader of men.

Theodore had planned this to see if his son would be duly impressed. And he was.

"You're impressed? Most are when they see the city from above," Theodore said. "I and my men built it all from scratch and now that you have come of age, I want you to know it. In fact, more than that. I want you to have it, to receive it from me as your bequest. The time is now."

Andrew took a step back, faltering, almost teetering off the parapet.

"You know that soon. This will be yours as my son, my first seed," Theodore said.

Andrew was in awe, worried, striding the parapet as he continued to look below.

He'd experienced the city from ground level in the past week, but to witness it from above in the tower was truly breathtaking. Here was a vast city indeed, inhabited by people who looked like mere specks of dust working in the industries that his father had created. But he did not appear ready or willing to take the colossal task from his father. He was too young and unready.

"It is true then, Father," he ventured. "People keep saying one thing to me over and over."

"And what do they say about me, Son?"

"That you are a progressive man. I see it all now."

Theodore's head nodded. But he held a knowing look as if to say, *ah, you only think you do.*

Like others, Andrew had known the city of Teleos was impressive, but to see it from so high above highlighted the work and dedication his father and his loyal men had put in to building this metropolis. Andrew had been away at his education, of course, staying with a family in a far city.

Now, he had all the academia he required under his belt. But he still lacked what every leader required: vision, leadership, and the staunch determination he had hoped would slowly but surely rub off on him so that one day, when his father was in his dotage, he could take over the city.

The words 'soon' and 'the time is now' had made Andrew flinch.

He did not hope it would be 'soon' his own. No boy would hope for that. Not so young. He had a lot of living to do—living that did not involve noise and dust, and no doubt argumentative men.

"Father." Andrew turned around slowly to look his father in the eyes. "I think I understand you right, but why would you give all of this to me? Surely, there are others worthier than I?"

"How do you mean?" Theodore inquired, seeming a little put out. "You do not want it?"

"Of course, I do," he placated, tongue in cheek and with a blush of redness down his sheepish face. "I mean that I have not been here at your side. I did not choose to leave the school and come to aid you in the construction when you invited me. That is all I mean. Of course, I want it, but I don't deserve—I mean, not yet. Perhaps later, I shall show how I deserve it from you."

He was playing at being humble, not wanting the great gift bestowed upon him quite yet!

"Give me a decade or two, good Father, then I shall have shown you how I deserve it."

"Ah, hush. 'Deserving' has nothing to do with it, my son. Deserving means getting a gift. This is your birthright. Besides, you are here to learn how to deserve it *now.*"

Andrew smiled, though it was a nervous look. He had to earn it? Oh...

Andrew had not given up his arguing yet. He would try again.

"Well, in decades, when you can no longer look after it, I shall be more mature and more worthy and more experienced... You have done a perfect job over the years, and you are still standing strong," Andrew explained. "I should be glad to accept it then, when you can no longer do the work. Then, when you are on your deathbed, Father, you may count on me. As your followers say, Father, you are a very progressive man, and you have much more to achieve."

It sounded like one of his typical get-out clauses. Andrew was not here to 'earn' anything, it seemed. He was merely here to ogle what his father had achieved, in the hopes his father would carry on achieving it for as long as possible so that one day, Andrew could merely inherit it when the great city was fully running itself and was less reliant upon a leader to steer the workers.

And at that stage, every bit of work would have been done.

"Father, the industry you made has afforded you to buy this entire city, and now you wish to hand it all to me." Please don't get me wrong, Father, and I'm thrilled by what you suggested, but you have created a city that every other aspires to. And your work ethic is what they aspire to.

"And now you want to hand it over to me, a lazy juvenile who has not laid a single stone in this city, or anywhere else for that matter." Look at you, Father. *You* are Teleos. Teleos is you.

"You are everything this city stands for!"

Theodore sighed deeply. This wasn't a decision he'd come to overnight. No, this was something Theodore had dwelled on, spending many a sleepless night mulling over his decision. There could be only one heir to what he had created with the help from his people and his famed progressive nature. It was time to be progressive enough to hand it down the generations!

"Son, I admire your words and yes, you are partly right in what you say," he replied. "But you are my son, my very creation, and everything I am, you are too. Take today, for instance."

"You came here still asking for my permission to talk to me," this being despite my written invitation many weeks ago. My own son asking me to spare some time. That cannot be right. But at a similar age, I would have done the exact same thing. Some may question the logic, but that shows respect, Andrew, and respect plays a huge role for when you take over the reins.

"And you will, Son, and soon. I have every confidence in you improving and even expanding this great city if you so choose. It will be down to you to make all decisions. Progressive or not!"

"I am your son, but I do not think I can do half the things that you do, Father," Andrew said.

He was looking glum by now. His father was barely hearing anything he had to say. "I hardly have any experience with managing industry or cities and I would not want to destroy what you have worked so hard to build up. I could bring it all crashing down in a manner of speaking."

"Yes, Teleos is my sweat and blood," Theodore said. "And I have done so much to bring it to where it is now. But you have my blood running through your veins, Andrew. You are my son, and you take after me, as I have just said. You already show me I have chosen correctly."

"But Father, will the people even want to hear from me?" Andrew asked, fear trembling in his voice clearly now. "When I rule, will they obey me? Will I gain the same respect as yourself?"

"Andrew, you are my son," Theodore cried. "Take charge *and rule,* for the sake of the gods!"

He sounded angry. His voice was shaking, and the ceiling echoed back his irate words.

What on earth was amiss with the boy Andrew that he was being so argumentative? He was driving the usually placid Theodore to become irate. He had not wanted to force the role on his own son; Andrew should have been down on his knees, thanking him profusely!

To inherit the father's wealth was simply how it was meant to be. Every family did this.

At last, Andrew had fallen silent. He picked at his hands and stared at the ground as he heaved a great sigh. This visit had already gone badly, not at all as he must have planned or hoped.

His father spoke again. "When you do this, everything will fall into place. Son, just remember this. I would never put you in a position where I thought you may struggle, especially not into a position so great as the one I have offered. And there is an advantage to you doing it while I live."

"But Father," Andrew said after a long stretch of silence. "What would you do while I am... while I am in charge of Teleos? Where will you be? Will you be close by if I need your advice?"

"Of course, Son. I will always be there for you and will steer you in the right direction if needed, but I have lots of other responsibilities to take care of," Theodore said. "So, I need someone I can trust to steer the ship while I attend to these other tasks. I trust you. Though after all your arguments and what ifs, and protestations, and your vagueness, I no longer know why."

Andrew thought it over and continued staring in awe at what his father had achieved over the years. It was truly spectacular; the buildings were tall and huge like Andrew could only dream of. Given the same opportunity, most would have jumped at the chance to run this great city.

He certainly didn't want to disappoint his father or the people of Teleos. In short, the boy Andrew had little self-belief to take on a sizeable task like this one. He would surely mess it up.

"I understand, Father, but I also hope you understand my apprehension, too. This is huge, not just for me, but for us both, and I don't want to destroy what you and many others here have achieved. But I truly appreciate the confidence you have shown in me. I will try my best."

"Nonsense, Andrew. You remind me so much of myself in my younger days and look at what I have achieved. Look at this! Look where we now stand!" Theodore said, circling his arms in front of him. "So, there is no reason you cannot do the same and achieve more. Look, Son, beneath me I have a truly dedicated team, a team that I trust, and these people will be here to do likewise for you. They will assist in every way and help lighten the load somewhat."

Once again, Andrew pondered what the great man had said.

"Then so be it, Father. I appreciate your words of advice and with trepidation and support from your people, I look forward to leading Teleos forward. I accept."

Theodore, overwhelmed by his son's reluctance and lack of confidence in his own abilities, had come to a rash decision. "Andrew, I have decided," he said. "Tomorrow will be the day."

His son's face turned a deathly white, every limb trembling.

Smiling, his father walked out of the penthouse, leaving Andrew to himself.

The poor boy was left quivering in his own skin.

Andrew had surely known that his father was rich, but he couldn't have known he was *as* rich as he'd discovered during his short time at Teleos. The city was something out of this world, and to build such would have taken a serious amount of money. Growing up, the textile industry had been all Andrew had ever known his father to do all his life. Andrew had visited the business a few times and always was treated like royalty, each loyal worker going out of their way, treating him with the same respect they showed for his father, Theodore.

Whether it was a sign of genuine hospitality, Andrew certainly welcomed it.

What he never imagined or gave much thought to was him heading even the company on behalf of his father. Now, there was talk of the city too!

After what seemed like a few hours of staring and thinking, Andrew walked out of the penthouse, having decided to do what his father had asked of him, and to give his best.

The reassurances his father had given soon swept aside the feeling of initial shock.

And like his Father had said, he would never put his son in a position where he felt he was uncomfortable or incapable. So, he would need to trust in his father's judgment and take in all he said. This would give him the drive he needed to take on his new role. And what a role that was.

In the short time since he had moved to Teleos, he had done nothing but wander about the city streets and walls, carefully taking down all the notes he deemed necessary for future reference.

He wanted to learn, jotting down the names of certain individuals and what their roles were within the textile mill. He had written what each gigantic machine did, and even the cost of downtime if, for some reason, a particular machine malfunctioned. Andrew was covering all bases, and his enthusiasm soon became apparent amongst the people of Teleos.

But this had been an enthusiasm for the weaving of cloth, nothing more than that.

Andrew had lacked nothing. Even though he had never got to meet his mother, he had also never felt as though anything was missing. His father had provided for him all that he needed—materially and emotionally—at the click of a finger.

People could say it was easy to be a provider if you owned such superior wealth, but his father was always there for Andrew, regardless, even when the boy chose a seemingly wayward path.

"Excuse me. Would you like to return to your quarters now?" Michael asked, shaking Andrew out of his thoughts. "Your father has set for tomorrow to be the day you take over from him and it will be busy indeed. I suggest you take some rest now."

"Thank you, Michael," Andrew said kindly. As he walked out of the room and down the stairs, he looked lost in thoughts, no doubt continuing to think about what he had seen.

No doubt he would also have considerable trouble sleeping tonight under the pressure of what was to come in the morning. So instead, he headed to his father's room.

"Michael, would it be possible to see my father before I head to my room? There are a few things I feel I still need to ask him and to discuss before tomorrow."

"Of course. But your father and many others from the city are currently in a meeting. We can head to his room and check if it's convenient. You will, after all, be in the chair tomorrow."

Michael soon ushered Andrew into the grand bedroom with its opulent fabrics that his men had woven for him, and at the far side was a set of fine chairs around a rectangular long table.

"Father, what would you—" Seated at the head of the table where meetings were held with leaders in the city, Theodore rose his right hand, signaling for Andrew to fall quiet again.

On his left were two gray-haired men with scrolls and ink, and on his right was Uriel.

He was 'the fire guy', as Andrew liked to call him.

The gray-haired man closest to Theodore looked for permission to carry on with the discussion, which Theodore acknowledged with a nod of his head.

"The people in the east of Teleos, Havilah, have found even more gold flowing in their city," the gray-haired man said. "They reported this to their city leader, and he had them store up the gold in the bunkers. There is enough gold to fill it from top to bottom and no room to move."

"Not just gold, but many other fine metals," the second man pitched in quickly. "It still flows as we speak. No one could have guessed so much wealth was there."

"Hmm," Theodore said. "And the other cities?"

"Faring well, Master," the first said. "The factories in the areas are all working well, and everything is in order. I have no reports of breakages or losses of men."

"Uriel, you need to order the firing of the gold," Theodore said.

"Yes, Master."

"But, Master," the second man interrupted again. "The reserves are overflowing, and the people are wondering when we will begin to use this gold, and when we will likely explore other metals to make *our* town more valuable."

"Andrew here will handle that," Theodore said. "He starts tomorrow. Hear that, Andrew?"

There was a deep silence in the room as everyone present turned around to look at Andrew.

He panicked at first, but somehow found the courage to walk to the table and take a seat.

"He is taking over control of the entire city from tomorrow, as I have some things to sort," Theodore said. "Those things can no longer wait, so, as of tomorrow, Andrew calls the shots."

"B-but, Master," the first man said, anxious, turning to Andrew. "I mean no offense, young one, but you know nothing about the way we operate things. You have barely even a week accrued with us and not more than three days of it at the factory that runs this city."

Theodore stayed quiet and looked on at Andrew. How would he respond?

"Thank you for your concern, but I will lead just like my father because I have his blood running in my veins," Andrew said boldly. Theodore gently nodded his head in approval.

He looked pleased, almost puffing himself up to hear his son's sure words for a change.

Perhaps all he had needed to do to make the boy into a man was to give him responsibility.

"Besides, I have assigned you all as my right-hand men," Theodore said. "You know how I do all that I do, so you will guide him when I am attending to other diverse matters, and you will show him the same level of respect that you show me. For which I am truly grateful."

"Yes, Master," the first man said.

"I am not leaving the city." Theodore assured he would always be here. I simply need to give my son control because he is my son, and I have other projects that need attending to.

"Yes, Master." This time, both men spoke.

"Thank you, Father," Andrew said, pushing his chair back and leaving the room.

The rest of the night was cold, almost chilly. Andrew turned and turned in his bed before finally planting his feet on the cold bedroom floor, rubbing his hands aggressively through his hair.

"Why can't I sleep? It's all right for you," he said to the old sundial down in the courtyard as he gazed out into the blackness. "You watch the passing of the hours with no care in the world. Well, let me tell you something. You're no help. All you do is while away the time, second by second, bringing me closer to my big day. Do you know that? I dislike you."

Andrew took in a deep breath and lifted his legs back onto the creaking, wobbly bed.

"Goodnight," he said to nothing in particular, pulling the coarse camel hair blanket over his head. Soon, he was snoring. It was a fitful sleep in which his body was never still.

Chapter 2: The Day Hath Come

The day of the assignment seemed like any other in the textile mill, especially one of this magnitude. Gigantic machines operated by the skilled and experienced, worked away, creating their own distinct noise, adding to the wealth of Theodore and the city of Teleos. It was no doubt an impressive sight, and very soon, it would be under Andrew's control. Busy, hot, yet cheerful.

This day was filled with excitement and an amount of apprehension within the city.

This was the day on which the respected Theodore would hand over the running of the city to his son, Andrew. Rumors had started, quickly spreading throughout the neighborhood and while most within the city were not too concerned about the decision, a few inhabitants doubted Andrew's ability, fretting that there would soon be a gradual decline in their wonderful city.

Theodore had called for a meeting with all the leaders and heads of every city function.

Now, in the early morning and only shortly after the sun had risen, each one had turned out immaculately, looking as clean as could be, each wearing a fine cream ceremonial robe they only took out on special occasions. The handing over of the city to the leader's heir was such a date.

Andrew had never seen them all in one place before.

Standing in front of the assembled group and upon an impressive dais, Theodore looked down upon his loyal men, ones who had served him well throughout his years. He waved to a few.

Andrew sat with Michael—Theodore's right-hand man—just to Theodore's right.

"It's such an honor to stand here in front of you all, within this impressive hall that many of you helped build," voiced Theodore. "Each and every one of you has played a part in making Teleos the envy of all, and I cannot thank you enough for your continued support and dedication.

"Your understanding and your perseverance have succeeded in creating this wonderful city that so many years ago was just a dream," Theodore said.

He was looking over the assembled people in the great hall; many stood wide-eyed, agog at their master. Ripples of whispers occasionally passed through. "So progressive!" they repeated.

"You all know this hall is only used for what I would call *special events*, and today does not differ from the last. Many of you are aware that a mere week ago, my son Andrew," Theodore said, pointing to his son, "came here to Teleos for the very first time in his young life."

There was no sound in the hall. No shifting of legs, no deep breaths, no clearing of throats.

Just hundreds of men looking straight ahead to hear what their revered master had to say.

"Some may already have seen him these last few days. Some may have seen him in his younger days on the occasional visit to previous establishments within the textile mill.

"But this time, Andrew has come to Teleos to stay, not to leave. He is my only son, the first seed, and I have now planted him here in Teleos to grow," Theodore said. "I understand there may be rumors circulating about the future of Teleos, so it's only fair to make an - official announcement quashing any differences of opinion and any confusion that I hear runs rife."

Theodore looked at his son.

Andrew turned his head slightly toward his father, giving a half hearted smile.

"From today, Andrew will take over the control of the entire city of Teleos. He shall take over the mill and the waterworks, and the great city itself. He may call the decisions in every part."

Without prompting, a loud round of applause mixed with murmuring followed Theodore's statement, but it all died down as soon as their leader raised his hands.

"He's young, but he's keen, and I see the same drive and determination I saw in myself those many years ago. He knows a lot of what he needs to know. My son will need each of you to pick him up if he falls," Theodore said. "You will be there for him if needed, and you will guide him. I understand it's a major change, but I will always be on hand to help, support and advise throughout. And between us all, we can achieve even greater things."

"Yes, Master," the men chorused in unison.

"Thank you for your time. I know each one of you will support Andrew through the coming years. Oh, and please let it be known that I shall school Andrew only to work in the old ways, and you all know what this entails. So, please welcome Andrew, the future of Teleos."

Again, there came another round of applause and this time, the focus was on Andrew, the son of their prominent leader. Then followed the deathly silence that Andrew was no doubt expecting.

He seemed to have fallen into deep thought at his father's mention of the old ways. His expression seemed to say, *what did Father mean by that? Of course, old ways are all we have!*

"Andrew, if you would like to say a few words to these wonderful people," Theodore announced. Michael stood, gesturing for the young leader to join his father, also placing a big, reassuring hand on the young man's shoulder as he led him to Theodore.

Smiling apprehensively at his father, Andrew swallowed hard.

Now, he was facing the eager and friendly audience, though some eyed him askance.

"You'll have to excuse me, but this is the first time I have stood before such a large gathering, and I have to say you all look wonderful." Andrew swallowed again. "I-I understand the respect each of you has for my father, and I hope... no, I know, you will respect me the same way."

Andrew looked at his father with a hint of what appeared to be glee. Was he actually enjoying his oration? Was he reveling in how the people stared at him up on the dais in wonder?

"So, I thank you all for welcoming and accepting me into your... *our* wonderful city. I promise to do my utmost by you, to make Teleos a pleasanter, happier, and more prosperous place." He stepped back to another round of applause, handing over to Theodore.

"Thank you, Andrew, and thank you all for the tremendous support you show to me day in, day out. I will now hand you over to Michael, who will explain the agenda for the next meeting."

Another round of applause, and Theodore placed his hand on his son's shoulder, leading him off the stage, letting Michael do what he did best—being a spokesman for Theodore.

"That was excellent, Son. See, you have what it takes. I knew that would be the case. You have already begun to learn from me. But I apologize for exposing you to such pressure."

"I expected it, Father. I bear no malice."

They laughed like two men for the first time, rather than as a man and an uncertain boy.

"Come along. We have a meeting with the elders within the textile factory," Theodore said, showing Andrew into another room, much smaller than the great hall, but equally impressive.

Many tables here were laid out with precision, each with a drinking goblet, a small plate of fresh fruit, and a cloth, as if they had come here for a meal. But they had not.

They were here for discussions of important things, but as they talked, they would eat.

Theodore led Andrew to the top of the table, two chairs placed next to each other on a small platform again. The room soon filled with those of authority within Teleos, taking up their usual positions around the long table. There was so much to discuss with each head of works introducing themselves, what their job entailed, how long they had worked in the craft.

All the time, the young leader scribbled down more and more notes on his scroll. The sound of the nib scratching on coarse parchment filled the air each time the men stopped talking.

Theodore sat alongside, watching his young son take it all in. The meeting lasted a full shift, and soon, noon had arrived.

"I think that's it," Theodore said at last. "Unless anyone has anything else for us?"

Theodore looked at each person, then at Andrew.

"No? Then humble thanks to you all, gentlemen," Theodore said, rising from his chair, and each person filed through the doorway.

"Father," Andrew said once the meeting was over, now standing next to his father and bowing his head. "You are a great man, and it is an honor to be your son."

Theodore was moved by what Andrew had said, his hand flying to his heart.

"You are empowered to think and create, just like I do," Theodore said. "Everything I have, the entire city, I have given to you. Control, lead, guide, designate. All will obey because you are my son. You have seen this for yourself. All decisions are now yours to take!"

"Thank you, Father," Andrew said. "I will not fail you."

"I know," Theodore said. He looked away, signaling for someone to come closer. "This is your right-hand man, Phillip. He will be your direct guide. Any problems you encounter, or any advice you need, you go to Phillip straightaway. Or, if you choose, you can come to m e."

"You are welcome, sir," Phillip, a young man in his prime, said as he approached Andrew. He gave a quick bow with his upper body, a sign of deference.

"Phillip knows everything about Teleos and about the factory that we run," Theodore continued. "And don't forget, when you need answers, no matter how trivial you think they are, you can come to me, or may simply speak with him."

"Yes, Father," Andrew said. "Thank you."

"Enjoy your first day of work," Theodore said. "I will leave you in Phillip's capable hands." Turning around, he headed toward his chambers with his right-hand men following closely.

"What would you have me do, sir?" Phillip asked, not looking Andrew in the eyes.

"Oh no! Please, call me Andrew."

"Then I shall, Andrew."

"I would like to go to the factory to check on how well the gold is being worked," Andrew continued. "If we could go there first."

"Yes, of course, Andrew. Please, if you would," Phillip said, motioning for the new leader to follow. "It's a long walk, but it will give you an idea of the masterpiece your father has created. I understand you will work only in the old ways..."

Again, young master Andrew looked a little perplexed.

Walking alongside his now right-hand man, Andrew took in the intricate detail of the city. He knew his father was a clever man, but to see his vision firsthand and up close was astounding. Theodore had designed the city with simplicity in mind, as well as building it with such immense depth and thought. Many of the regularly used buildings were interconnected by four equally spaced entrances, evenly distributing the foot traffic and preventing unnecessary queuing.

A simple, but clever idea.

Phillip would point out buildings he thought were of importance, and Andrew had taken in his father's words, asking Phillip whenever he felt the need to know about a certain feature.

"What are your thoughts so far, Andrew? I know you have spent an entire week here, but I doubt you will have had the time to venture this far into the city."

"My word! It truly is something special. It's no wonder Teleos is the envy of those around us. And no, I never came this far into the city. I have spent most of that time sticking close to my father's mansion. I mean, I saw it from my rooms, but to see it up close is quite another matter."

"It certainly is, and even though I have been here for so many years, it's still breathtaking. But it's also a simple city to live in. Everything is where you expect it to be, and the road network is foolproof. Designed on a grid system. It will take you no time at all to master it, Andrew."

"Yes, I noticed each street had a number, followed by a letter. Simple, really."

"I suppose you know about the connection running between the factory and Theodore's mansion?" Phillip said.

"Yes, Father had mentioned it, but I have yet to see it. Maybe some other time?"

"Of course. We'll have plenty of time. Plenty for everything."

Theodore's mansion was enormous, with separate annex housing for those who looked after the grounds and the upkeep of this imposing building, with lesser houses within close proximity. These were owned by those close to Theodore and those at the top tier of the Teleos hierarchy.

A sort of community within a community if you like.

Andrew had stayed at his father's home since arriving in the city and couldn't believe the masterpieces hanging from the vast walls, including beautiful works of art collected through time and kept in the mansion, as though it were a museum. Tapestries from bygone days were his specialty, and these hung on brass rods on every expanse of wall. There were statues too, antiquated and representing mighty fights between the gods and their minions.

Finally, there were the ancient carvings and books by elderly scribes of centuries gone by.

It was one of the things that had amused Andrew the most when he moved to Teleos.

"Here, my father has created a new city, a modern place, no less. They say he is a progressive man, a man of the future! Yet look around! He persists in filling this city with the antiquated," he had said to himself one day, walking room to room and eyeing the wall hangings and sculptures, none of which he believed could have any relevance today. He laughed at how his father had filled the place with old things, while proclaiming to look ahead into the future!

In secret, he laughed at his father and his followers.

"Alas, my father is living in the olden times," he quipped. "It's a good thing I am here!"

But he had no idea of what was to come!

"Finally! Here we are, Andrew," Phillip said. "Welcome."

Looking around, Andrew saw nothing but a well-structured small space.

It was nothing to look at—no opulence here.

There was barely even room enough for two within the plain-walled tiny space.

"Here, we can observe each process within the factory from a solitary position," voiced Phillip. Sitting upon one of the tabletops was a screen of some kind, lit with bright colors behind some sort of gigantic shiny sheet material in which Andrew could see his own reflection.

There were many odd buttons to press in front of the numerous screens. They came in a multitude of colors and hues, each glowing on and off, on and off...

Andrew glanced at each screen, displaying a different area within the complex.

"We can press a button and speak to the workers," said Phillip, as Andrew's eyes grew so wide they threatened to tumble from his head.

"And they will hear what I say?" Andrew asked. "Without delay? But how?"

"Yes, it's instant. Watch." Phillip leaned onto a desk, reaching for a small device he called a 'microphone'. "Response team. Are you on?"

"On and ready to go, sir!" a voice echoed back immediately. Andrew jumped sky high!

"And these men are placed around the complex?" Andrew asked, his eyes popping.

"Yes, your father insisted we place individuals at potentially vulnerable places within the factory. So, if there was an issue, they would be on hand to react immediately."

What on earth was this place? Phillip walked over to the side of the room, pushing a few of those peculiar buttons for himself and as he did, lights came on and a large section of the wall slid to the left, giving way to a huge glowing panel stretching the entire length of one side.

It was like the little screens, only fifty times as large and impressive.

"We call it *glass*," he said. "And these things, the knobs, *plastic*. Materials of the future. Materials of progression. But you need not worry so much about them since you will be working in the old ways."

What? Andrew's face was a picture!

Andrew walked over to the shiny wall, and the view was unbelievable. His jaw dropped.

When he placed his hands upon the 'glass' wall, close-ups came of different factory sections.

"From in here, you have complete control of everything within the textile mill," Phillip explained further. "We have men to enforce any instructions you give from here, and you will be able to see it being done, too. And over here, you can print a report. These are your father's new ways—well, just a few of them. But don't forget your instruction is to work *only in old ways.*"

He now pointed to a strange machine with thin parchment sticking out from the top.

"*Printer*, we call that," said Phillip. Andrew now had to pull over a heavy wood chair and sit.

Otherwise, he would have fallen over with the shock of it all. *Plastic? Glass? Printer?*

A secret little room from which they could spy on every corner and every worker of the mill?

Beyond belief! Beyond possibility! Well, so much for working in the old ways!

What the people said was clearly true, and Andrew had to swallow all his doubts.

His father was indeed the progressive man of the future. Everyone had always said he was.

Andrew had nothing to say anymore. All hints of mockery of his father's seemingly antiquated ways were gone. His face no longer smiled in derision at ancient surroundings.

On balance, this was perfect. His fingers danced upon the vivid buttons in a spectrum of hues, and they each gave off a vivid glow; everything was new to him here.

Well, this was at complete odds with the ancient fabrication of the buildings and the slow way of life from which he had come. How *did* they come to have such marvels here?

It was evident his father had more talents hidden up his sleeve than he had credited to him!

There were no ancient scrolls here, no wall hangings, no old and dusty parchments and quills.

"It seems as if Father has thought of everything. Even small details are covered by something he introduced. But I have to say, this technology is eons beyond anything I saw before."

"Oh, yes, and more, Andrew. Your father is forever trying to push Teleos forward. He has some way of getting a hold of such gadgets. And dare I say it, but you have a lot to live up to. But don't forget, you have talented people around you, ones that will help you succeed.

"We still work in the ways of the old school but taking advantage of the very newest tools. There is nothing you will be left wanting. But you must follow your father's ways. He is wise."

"Thank you, Phillip. I just don't want to let my father and the people of Teleos down," Andrew said. He looked down through the glass and noticed Uriel in a room, heating gold.

Andrew wanted to keep his father happy, just as he had heard, but he also was going to find himself tempted by the many wonders he was seeing with his own eyes. He was tempted by the new.

The gold had his heart thumping.

"What if we were to build an entire palace in Teleos with all of this gold?" Andrew suggested.

It was clear he was already getting grandiose ideas, seeing so much of the yellow metal for the first time. Plus, no doubt his father's 'technology' could work wonders with this molten metal! He was racing ahead, thinking of the many marvels they would be able to conjure up.

"We use it for special occasions," Phillip said. "Maybe we could build a bunker beneath to store valuables of the city. A metal-lined room to keep it free from break-ins. Keep it simple..."

A metal room? Is that all? Andrew's expression seemed to cry out.

If his father had been able to take a leap of faith and bring technology into the ancient city of Teleos, then clearly, his father was truly forward thinking and open to all manner of progress!

"That would be a good idea, Phillip," Andrew said. "However, according to what you have said, we have so much gold that even building a palace would take only about half of what we have stored up. Is that not so? Do we not need something... more progressive?"

He liked that word now. And if he was taking over from his father, then surely, he too needed the workers to see he was moving ahead with the times. "Show me how much gold there is."

Phillip leaned forward and pressed a few buttons, bringing up the storage area on one monitor. "This is what we currently have in storage at the factory, but we have so much more stored within other facilities, waiting to be transported here."

"And all of this gold came only from Havilah?" Andrew asked.

"Yes," Phillip replied. "What you see on the screen all came in from Havilah."

"Hmm," Andrew said. "Tell me about security here at Teleos. What do we have in place, and who are our enemies?" As he asked his many questions, the phrase *building a palace* had become stuck in his head. Perhaps that was not a bad idea! Building a palace! Hmm!

Phillip adjusted his stance.

"We have not had any strain in our relationship with people outside of Teleos in recent times. In fact, it's quite the opposite. There is the odd skirmish, but nothing directed at Teleos, and usually between lesser forces trying to gain ground on others."

"And before then? Anything worthwhile, considering?"

"The city of Golgotha, not too far from here, tried to break our forces a couple of times in the past, no doubt trying to steal from our reserves," Phillip said. "Of course, with more facilities like you see here, we have ways of knowing what our enemies are up to. We can often anticipate when they will show up and what their plans may be. Your father has planned everything with great care. He knows what is afoot and knows ahead of all the dangers. He is a shrewd man.

"That is why when we do something new, we mostly still do it in his old way."

Andrew appeared confused. "Why do something new in an old way?" he asked, scratching his head. "Why not do the new in the new way? You are making my head spin."

"Because your father, while he might like technology, loves the old way. It is as it is. But do not underestimate the use of the new for the purposes of the old. But as for actually using the new, very few of us have permission."

And that was that. For now, anyway. Andrew would have to stick with it, though it must have seemed strange to be the one in charge and yet to be told he could only work in limited ways.

He looked back at the monitor, studying the storage area on the glowing screen.

Were there more technologies of this sort?

And they could use them for the treatment and security of the gold?

And for security in general?

"Enemies don't die, Phillip," he said. "As long as there is still gold in here," Andrew continued, pointing at the screen, "then they will return. Think about it. It's no secret the wealth here at Teleos, and who's to say these smaller cities aren't collaborating with others?"

"I see your concern, Andrew, but I doubt many would try to take on our might. They have never known of our technological advantage so they are afraid of our unusual capabilities."

There was some silence before Andrew shook off his thoughts.

"Anyway, I will show you more of the factory and go through some of the more important aspects before we head back," Phillip said, leading the way.

"Son!" Theodore exclaimed when he saw Andrew walking into his chambers. "You have done very well! From the moment you took the stage and faced our people, I knew I had made the right choice."

Andrew walked briskly and knelt before his father.

"I would not have done so if you did not believe in me, Father," Andrew said with a weak smile. He'd had a long day, and the mental work was a bit heavy and foreign for him, so he was glad to be back in his father's home.

"You have made me proud," Theodore said.

"Thank you, Father."

"Leave us," Theodore said to Phillip and the other men in the room. "We will send for you when we have finished discussing."

The men took quick bows and soon, just as Theodore and Andrew remained in the room.

"What did you learn today?" Theodore asked his son as they walked to the end of the room to a mighty window overlooking the city.

"So many things, Father," Andrew said. "Our land is blessed, so blessed!"

Theodore smiled. "Of course it is. It is my creation, and I put my all into it. Each and every detail, which I'm sure you will notice over time, was carefully thought out."

"Yes, Father. I have seen some of your ideas already and discussed each with Phillip. But in general, none of the people lack anything that they need, and the factory is running just fine," Andrew said. He did not know how to begin mentioning the so-called *technology* of the place.

He was too confused about it all, and about the 'use of the new for the ways of the old.'

Or whatever it was that Phillip had been saying. He'd already forgotten, his mind running riot with a million *brand new* ideas for putting the gold and the technology to good use.

"Very good. I expect nothing else from my people," said his father, though by now, Andrew had quite forgotten what they'd been talking about. His head was somewhere in the clouds, dreaming of all the impossible things he could achieve by innovation...

The father and son stayed watching over the city until something caught Andrew's attention, drawing him even closer to the window.

"What's that?" Andrew asked.

"Where?"

"Over there. Like a patch of land with a very bright light."

Andrew pointed to the extreme of the city.

Theodore stayed quiet, looking straight ahead. His face had fallen; he looked somber.

"Father, can you see it?"

Still no response.

"Father?" Andrew turned to look at his father, wondering why he did not get a response.

"Of the entire city of Teleos," Theodore said. "If you walk into any house and knock, you would be accepted and treated well."

"Yes, I know," Andrew replied.

"And here in the mansion, there is nothing that you may need that you would not find. Am I correct?"

"Yes, Father."

"You also have a lot of work to do, and you will have the final say on any issue that surfaces. And most importantly, the entire city looks up to you now."

Andrew was getting a bit impatient, wondering where the conversation was going.

"Yes, Father, I am aware of this," he said.

"Then you have no business with that particular building on the outskirts of Teleos," Theodore replied firmly. "Remember that. Yes?"

Andrew was surprised and tried to hide it, but his father noticed everything.

"This may come as a surprise to you because, like many of the people in Teleos, you may wonder why I would stop you from visiting the brightest building in all Teleos.

"But you see, there is more to it than meets the eye. That bright building contains doom and suffering, and no one ever goes there," Theodore said. "You must never be found there and under no circumstance must you go anywhere near there. Don't even *talk* about the bright building. Just remove it from your thoughts. Banish it from your mind. This bit of advice is one of the most important if you are to become my successor."

Andrew swallowed hard. "Yes, Father."

Theodore stayed quiet for some time, father and son staring out across the city.

"Son, whatever you take away from this day, never forget my words about the bright building," Theodore said, never moving his gaze from the large window.

"Father, I thank you for your advice, and I promise to never venture to that side of the city."

Theodore didn't reply, and Andrew left for his own quarters. Night was falling upon the city.

Exhausted, Andrew bathed, then sat in the most comfortable chair, his mind racing from the day's events. Looking around the room, he caught a glimpse of his old parchment notes and quill, deciding to add what his father had said earlier. Turning the pages, Andrew found the last entry and scribbled an asterisk-shaped symbol on the sheet to highlight the point.

"I need to think about this," Andrew said to himself and wrote more.

'Spoke with Father upon return to room. Noticed bright light within city when looking through Father's window. Asked what it was, but would not tell me. Finally, he told me to stay away from the bright building. Don't even mention it. BANISH BRIGHT BUILD-

ING. Didn't say why, but seemed a big deal. Father is clever, so I need to listen.

'Point noted. Long day, time for bed.'

Months passed by in the city of Teleos and each day, Andrew became more familiar with the running of the factory and the huge responsibility of steering the city in the right direction. Up to this point, Phillip had been a godsend, advising Andrew where he thought necessary and answering any question with clarity. Andrew still made a point of taking notes each day, quickly filling the large parchment sheets with relevant points and instruction, all written in ink with his ancient quill or nib. Over time, he had gained in confidence, leading the weekly meetings, but always with Phillip or his father at his side. A sort of safety net. But his mind was lately ill at ease.

The ever-increasing amount of gold was troubling Andrew. He'd been impressed on first setting eyes upon the amount in storage, and it was evident the neighboring cities were aware of the huge resources within Teleos. He was beginning to lose sleep over this; fearing another attack on the city, Andrew needed to convince his father to use the gold to build a mansion.

In due course, he produced a detailed assessment of the reasons it was a no-brainer.

"When the enemy comes, and I'm sure they will, they would never be able to take an entire building," Andrew had said. "We place the humongous golden mansion right where they can see it, as plain as day. We do not hide it—no, we put it right up front. Because what can they do?

"They can hardly build a furnace to melt something that reaches to the sky!"

"And that is not wrong, but the real gold the enemy wants is in your heart and your mind, not the physical gold of Teleos," Theodore often replied. "They crave our intellect more."

But his son did not let the matter lie, giving poor Theodore many sleepless nights over it, too. After all, had he not said he was handing the reins to his son?

Therefore, was it right of him to deny this idea? Would the boy ever let the matter lie?

Perhaps he should agree, see what came to pass in the fullness of time! This would show whether his son Andrew was capable of having worthy ideas or would take the whole kingdom down with him. So, finally, he found himself agreeing to build the mansion.

In fairness, Andrew stayed strong throughout the months of continuous labor—heating, melting, and molding—and finally, he had achieved his dream.

Theodore was a proud man, seeing what his son had achieved. Andrew had handled things even better than his father had imagined. The vast, golden-domed mansion ruled over Teleos.

Now, the other cities' leaders could come from afar to witness the splendor of it, but it was way too big for any to think of stealing. All in all, Theodore found it had been a good idea.

And in the process, he had witnessed his son growing in the confidence to lead and decide.

Theodore remained on the sidelines throughout, watching the young prodigy organize his men—even lending a hand where necessary. This earned Andrew so much respect amongst the people of Teleos. Andrew understood everything about the factory now.

He knew the entire process of production, and he had taken the learnings from this and had built another hospital for children. He knew each worker by their name and knew everything that was going on in the city. He was proving to be a leader at heart, pleasing Theodore, too.

Andrew continued to thrive, but his father was noticing a slight change in his son's demeanor.

It wasn't a great issue, but he would need to speak with Andrew.

"Something bothers you, son."

Theodore had made a point of catching up with Andrew the next morning.

"No, Father, everything is good," Andrew said. "Why do you ask? Has anyone said anything?"

"No, Son, I just see it. As yet, I don't know what, but there is something. I have noticed these last few days. Don't forget, we are all here to support you if you so choose."

Andrew paused, turning away from his father.

"I don't think I am as strong as you," Andrew started. "I am becoming lonely as I often need someone to speak with during my day. Please don't see it as a weakness, Father."

"Nonsense! You have me, Son," Theodore said. "Why would you need anyone else?"

"And you are more than enough for me, Father. I only need a companion. A good lady."

"Son, you are doing a wonderful job. Don't expect every day to be the same. We all have ups and downs; that's part of life. Just continue what you're doing. A woman would divert you."

Theodore gave Andrew's *problem* little thought and after more talk about work, the issue was dismissed. But for Andrew, this was a worry. Although he saw his father as a visionary man, Andrew believed not everything should be achieved alone. He saw that his father was wrong.

For all the new things his father was bringing into the city in secret, he had insisted Andrew stay working in the ways of the old. And surely, this would be a good argument to present.

A companion in life was a great thing, and he wanted one.

As such a renowned progressive and forward-thinking man, Theodore would agree in the end.

If Andrew could find himself a companion—a lovely woman, of course—then his father would certainly back him. He was sure of it. His father would agree with his way of thinking.

He would talk to Theodore again about this. And the next time, he would remind him that having a wife was something that people did who worked in the ways of the old.

Chapter 3: Amelia

Days after his father's chat, Andrew walked to check on something within the factory. "We need more hands in the weaving factory," Andrew said. "I said this some days ago."

"Yes, you did," Phillip replied. "It's already been arranged. A few new men and women are ready to work."

"Excellent, then please let me see them and speak with them."

Phillip led the way to a common room to meet the new workers, and seeing Andrew walk in, they jumped to their feet.

"Good day, sir," they chorused. Andrew responded kindly and had a quick headcount. Eleven in total, eight men and three women.

"You may introduce yourselves, please," Phillip said, nodding to his left. "We'll start with you on the end." One by one, each person gave a brief introduction, and Andrew could not help but notice the last lady to speak.

"My name is Amelia, daughter of late John and Beatrice Smith."

She took her seat again, listening to the remaining three men as they talked.

Andrew tried to stop staring at Amelia, but one thing was for sure, something about this woman drew him to her. She was beautiful, yes, but it was more than that.

"Okay, thank you all. You may now start," Andrew managed to say. For most of his day, Andrew couldn't stop thinking about Amelia, wanting to see her again.

Remaining quiet apart from a few words to Phillip, Andrew was lost in his thoughts and even when the day was over and he sat with his father, he was still distracted.

"Do you want to share what is on your mind?" Theodore said firmly, making Andrew jump out of his thoughts.

"Huh?"

"You have been distracted since the beginning of our meeting, Andrew. What is the matter? Your mind is elsewhere, Son."

Andrew smiled sheepishly and looked at his father.

"I have found myself a companion after all, Father," Andrew said. "Father, it's the old way."

Theodore's heart leaped. Andrew's performance had posed a worry to him ever since they had spoken about his need for someone to be with. The boy had been forever distracted.

"That is wonderful news, son," Theodore said against his better judgment. "Who is she?"

"Her name is Amelia, Father."

"Amelia?"

"Yes, Father. Amelia Smith. Her father was the late John Smith."

"Yes, I remember. He was a very faithful worker in my factory before an illness took his life. His wife died grieving shortly after."

"Hmm."

"They were good people, Andrew," Theodore said. "And I'm sure Amelia will carry on the great name. Where did you meet Amelia?"

"Phillip appointed her. She came to work at the weaving house, one of eleven extra bodies needed to cope with the amount of work. I don't know what it is, Father, but I'm drawn to her."

"Well, see what comes of it, Son. Just try your best not to get distracted. There is much we need to do." By that, he meant *there is much you, Andrew, need to do.*

"Thank you, Father!" Andrew exclaimed, clutching his father tightly. The joy Andrew felt knew no bounds. He continued the rest of the meeting with great enthusiasm, learning more of what his father knew and how he had kept the city standing for years.

Even though Theodore had supposedly handed over the running of Teleos to his son, he insisted they met every day, discussing the day's events and providing the support if needed.

Andrew looked forward to hearing stories of his father's deeds and learning important lessons from them. His father was, after all, a progressive man! His interest and investment in the technology had shown Andrew that. And let's not forget that Theodore had also allowed Andrew to build the massive golden palace in the city of Teleos, even though he'd disliked the idea.

He had also now allowed his son to take a companion; they were both moves to which he had objected. Yet to his father's joy, Andrew was building up the city even further.

Sure enough, in the weeks following, Andrew decided the time was right and he brought Amelia to his father, who blessed their union despite all his earlier reservations that she might distract Andrew from his colossal tasks. Theodore's mindset as the progressive man of whom everyone spoke had not stood in the way of his son accepting a companion and a wife.

He had quite come around to the idea, just as Andrew had envisaged and hoped.

Becoming closer to Amelia, Andrew thought it appropriate for her to no longer work in the factory, instead working alongside him, running the place and overseeing it all.

Amelia listened intently at his side, and Andrew likened it to when he'd followed his father on his daily rounds of the factory, learning from the great man himself.

"I wonder what my life would have been like if I had not found you," Andrew said to Amelia one evening, just as the factory was about to close for the day.

"And mine would have had no meaning if you had not come in when you did," Amelia replied. She was the most beautiful girl Andrew had ever seen, her long and silky brown hair falling over the bottom of her back. Before he met her, it was as though no other woman had existed. She was as rare as a gem, and a good home builder, the perfect wife and partner to assist Andrew both in the textile mill and in the growth of Teleos.

Many folks mistakenly thought Amelia to be timid, but she was a hard worker, and also a very smart one. Many times, Andrew asked Phillip to leave the room so he could think of a solution to a problem, and just sharing it with Amelia would make the problem go away, discussing with him until they came to a solution together.

"God blessed the day that I met you, Amelia." Andrew sang songs of love to her each day, and their marriage blossomed in a way that also gave Theodore peace and joy.

"Father, we are both here to learn from you!" Andrew said as he and his wife walked into the chambers of Theodore. "Though I believe we have come far in managing the business and Teleos, we have much to learn from you, especially in your progressiveness."

It had become routine for Amelia to come and see Theodore and learn from him as well, ever since she had joined the household, and Theodore was more than happy to accept her.

"I know you both think you do, but you must continue working together in wisdom," Theodore said. "Because the enemy, and there will be many, does not like to see us happy and peaceful. As for progression, continue to use the old in the old ways, and all is well."

That was not what Andrew wished to hear. It was clear that his father had so much technology at his fingertips, and so far, he had not learned anything about how to access it himself.

Just as he had persuaded Theodore to allow him to build the palace of gold and to take for himself a good lady wife, so too would he work on being allowed to use the new.

"What do you mean, Father?" Andrew adjusted himself on his chair, holding Amelia's hand.

"It's quite simple, Son. As long as you practice everything that I teach you, you will be protected from the intent of the enemy. This means adhering to our old customs and practices."

"Hmm." And that was why his father had the glass screens and the push-buttons, was it?

"So far, and it's clear to see, the entire city enjoys your leadership," Theodore continued. "Look how many gifts this household has received in thanks for you and your wife's works."

"Oh," Amelia chuckled, thoroughly enjoying her role of overseeing Teleos beside Andrew.

"Amelia." Theodore focused on his daughter-in-law. "I have heard nothing but good things about you. A representative from the new hospital said you spend your evenings there attending to the needs of the children and older women. You work in the old ways, giving your time."

"Yes, Father," Amelia said. "I only do it to help, and to relieve the nurses of their duties while I can. It only seems fair, as they do an amazing job for the whole of Teleos."

"They are very grateful for that," Theodore replied with a nod. "And you, Andrew. You raised salaries and included free meals twice a day for all workers."

"Yes, Father," Andrew said. "I noticed the meal they were getting in the past was not substantial enough when compared to the work that they do. And as Amelia said, they do a fantastic job for all at Teleos."

"Hmm," Theodore said. "You both are building my kingdom, *your* kingdom. You must remain focused and stay true to all you have learned. The people look up to you, and the energy they get to stay strong, they get from you both. You give them hope and keep their joy alive.

"Do not let that connection die, do you understand? As I say, stick to the old ways."

"Yes, Father, we do," Andrew said, speaking very confidently for himself and his wife. He knew these values and Amelia was learning and understanding them, too. "We will never disappoint you. You have done so much for us, and we owe you our devotion."

But as he said it, he was not sure sticking always to old practices was how his father had been running things. The old ways were all very well, but did they allow and encourage progress?

Yes, they could sit at the bedsides of the ill for days, for example, making sure they were able to breathe and were not getting any sicker. But they could also monitor them as they did the factory, couldn't they? With high-tech equipment, the sort his father used.

But as it was clear, his father was all for Andrew taking things slow, he would have to wait. Hopefully, in time, Theodore would share the secrets of the new things he had introduced.

"That is good," Theodore replied after a deep sigh.

They spent the rest of the night discussing the main developments within Teleos, with Andrew bringing his father up to speed on the progress within the city and beyond.

With careful consideration, the city had started supplying another on the outskirts with food and other farm produce, increasing their trade outside of Teleos for the very first time.

With advice from Phillip, they would soon set a date to officially and formally launch their golden mansion, and Theodore had also allowed Andrew to gain insight into one of his new technology projects. Spending hours with Phillip, Andrew discussed a means to convert areas with fast-flowing water into hydroelectric power plants, supplying electricity to the city by natural means rather than relying on a fuel to power the stations.

This meant they would never run out of electricity, and it was becoming a success too.

This had been another of Theodore's astounding new technology ideas, revolutionizing many aspects of life in Teleos that otherwise might have been too hard to live with.

By now, even the underground pipework for the water supply had been renewed in some kind of bright silvery metal, and Andrew had no idea how his father had arranged this either.

It seemed Theodore would only expose his new ideas in dribs and drabs.

One evening, when Andrew was preoccupied with an issue in the factory across the city, Theodore and Amelia were alone in the great residence.

"Amelia," Theodore said.

"Yes, Father." She was a gentle lady and spoke beautifully.

"You have lived in Teleos all your life, right?"

"Yes, Father. I was born here and lived with my parents here."

Taking her hand, Theodore led Amelia to the window.

"Look out at the extremes of the city," Theodore said, pointing toward the city gate at the brightly lit city. "You do know about that place, right?"

"Yes, I do." She looked at Theodore.

"Tell me. Tell me what you know and what you've been told."

"It is a place of destruction and evil and no one should be found around or within it."

Theodore nodded in approval.

"Listen to me," he said, turning around and looking directly at Amelia's eyes. "I have given this entire city to Andrew, your husband, and that means that he has been given the responsibility to care for Teleos, but also the power to demand what is and what is not."

"Yes, Father. We understand this."

"This is a responsibility that I have been carrying on my own shoulders for decades and I must say that it is no easy task," Theodore said. "As happy and peaceful as Teleos is, we have enemies who would stop at nothing to see us fall. And the more successful we become, which undoubtedly, we will, then the greater number of enemies we will have."

"Yes, Father, I am aware of this as well."

"Very good," Theodore said. "You are his wife, not just for the sake of it but for companionship, ease, and above all, assistance. It will not be easy for him to always be at the top of his game, you know? He relies on you to guide him in certain things. He has a tendency to race ahead and just do things without much thought. I tell him to stick to old ways. Can I be sure that he does? And will you promise to tell me if he is getting any ideas beyond his station?"

"Yes. I know there is a huge amount of pressure on someone as young as Andrew to continue where you left off. But I know he will do his best to make you a proud father. And yes, of course, I will tell you if I feel he is veering from the correct path. But if I may..."

She seemed hesitant.

"Yes, Amelia? Say whatever you wish to say to me. It all helps," he answered.

"I think in part, it is because he feels he must live up to your reputation as *a progressive man,* the man everyone speaks of and reveres, that he wishes to know the new ways.

"Because on the one hand, you work with the old ways we have inherited down the centuries but on the other, your workers show him the shiny plastic buttons and the big screens into the factory, to keep an eye on everything going on. And they tell him this is our future.

"They have shown him technology he has no context for. He does not know how you came by these things, so he thinks of the many ways to move forward with new technology, but you persist in telling him to stick to the old ways. He wants to move forward, as you did. Otherwise, how can he succeed in following after you?"

Theodore merely stroked his beard, thinking.

"So, when he seems to lose his way, what do you think is best for you to do?"

It was plain he had not heard a word Amelia had just spoken.

He had put her right back at the start.

"I shall remind him of the greater good and help him stay focused on what you have said."

"Wonderful. The moment you sense that things are out of your power, come to me. I will help. My door is always open, and please don't hesitate to approach me for advice, regardless of how small you may think it. And don't leave things too late. They will only spiral out of control and will be far more difficult to rectify. And yes, he must adhere to what I advise, the old ways."

"Of course, Father. Thank you for your support," Amelia said.

"The evil one will try and as much as you are indebted to Andrew, you are also indebted to his responsibility as leader of Teleos. Do you understand this? He must not be led astray."

"Yes, I do understand."

"I am always with both of you. You do not have to handle everything on your own. At your slightest inconvenience, find your way back to me."

"We will not forget this, Father," Amelia said. "Thank you."

Amelia retired for the night, leaving Theodore to himself.

He stood by a window, looking at the extreme of the city and the forbidden house. The lights shone very brightly, brighter than any other within the city of Teleos.

It had taken years of constant reminders to convince his people to understand the importance of looking away from it. It had taken years to understand the problems associated with this house and everything it represented, and he was glad that he had also been able to teach his son, Andrew, to look away too. Theodore had done his utmost to abandon that heinous place.

And he had to trust that in this, Andrew would not want to race ahead and try to do his own thing. If he did, he would not be following the old ways he was taught. If he did not follow the path taught to him by his father, Andrew might find himself tempted into forbidden places in more ways than one. This was the greatest fear of his father, Theodore.

Chapter 4: Autonomous Bots

"You do not want to leave home without having breakfast, Andrew," Amelia said with a wide grin. "Trust me. They say it's the most important meal of the day."

"Argh!" Andrew grunted. He'd spent hours throughout the night and into the early hours drafting plans for the factory and had finally come up with something.

He was sure this would change the city of Teleos forever.

"Come on!" Amelia continued, sitting at the far end of the large dining table in their private quarters. "The pancakes are to die for, and the tea is well brewed. You would love it. Come on."

"Fine!" Andrew finally gave in, placing his bundle of papers down on a couch and walking toward his wife. "Just one piece of pancake and I will be on my way."

"That's better than nothing," Amelia said, sipping her tea and smiling as she watched Andrew take a seat. The help in the house, Sharon, walked forward to pour the tea and serve Andrew a few pancakes and syrup.

"Thank you, Sharon," Amelia said. "That would be all for now."

"Alright, Madam Amelia."

Andrew delved into his meal, but stayed quiet.

"What is the matter now?" Amelia asked, putting her teacup down and leaning in, showing a genuine interest in her husband's concerns.

"Huh? Me?' Andrew muffled as he chewed on his pancake.

"Of course, you! Who else do you think I would be asking? You're as easy to read as an open book."

"Oh, well." Andrew heaved a deep sigh. "It has been six months since you came into my family and joined my father and myself in building Teleos and the textile factory."

"And" Amelia replied, even more curious given the way he had started.

"When you joined, we did a lot together and saw how rapidly the city grew under our watch."

"And?"

"I feel we need to do more, Amelia!" Andrew said, raising his hands in the air and heaving a deep sigh as he stared down at his meal. "There are neighboring cities we can sell to, more innovations, and more growth. It never really ends, you know? We must make progress."

Amelia smiled at her husband, knowing every issue was about improving life within Teleos.

"I hope you understand this. I mean, look at our work in the past few months," Andrew continued, now standing and pacing around the table. "We've assigned more staff to new departments in the factory that never even existed before. Not just our neighbors, but new cities.

"Cities from far away with whom we never imagined partnership with and now send men trooping into our city and even pay us for the training of their own men."

"Andrew."

"Now, the mansion of gold has become a tourist center, drawing in people from far and wide to pay to see it, and study it."

"Andrew—" Amelia tilted her head, waiting for Andrew to notice she was calling on him.

"Did you see that the leader of Justicia came by himself just to see our fine mansion of gold?

"He called Teleos 'the yellow city' and would have stayed even longer had his delegates not entreated him to return."

"Andrew!" Amelia dropped her teacup and shot him a stern look. "You need to relax! I swear you are becoming obsessed! All you ever speak of is work!"

Andrew heaved a deep sigh and stared down at the half-eaten pancake.

"All I am saying is," Andrew continued. "We have the capacity for more. We have the materials, the space, and the manpower, and also all we need to expand."

"And expand we shall," Amelia said quietly, standing from her seat ever so majestically and peacefully walking toward Andrew. "We also have all the time that we would ever need, so there isn't any reason in the world to rush, lest we make a costly mistake."

"Oh no, not a mistake. No, we would not make a mistake, but we need to act soon."

"Father would not want that, you know? He would call that *racing ahead.*"

"And even I would be devastated if anything goes wrong at all," Andrew said. "I do not plan to race ahead. I only plan to achieve great things with small strides."

"Then let us take it slow and allow what we have already built to grow," Amelia said. "Look at what we've achieved so far and appreciate that for now. Andrew, we don't want to overstretch our resources or people. We must work in the old ways. Father says so. Let's not rush ahead."

Andrew took some more time to eat his food in silence before he finally spoke, and Amelia went back to her seat after stroking her husband's back for a few minutes.

"I understand, Amelia. But Father is a fine one to talk about not rushing ahead, isn't he? He is the one with the new materials, his plastic, his glass, his magic buttons and his big screens, his printer, and his hydroelectric power! The people do not call him a progressive master for nothing. He has given control to me, so he says. An idea crossed my mind late last night. I can hardly wait for us to bring it to life," Andrew said. "*I* run this place now."

"Oh."

"Yes. I've planned to meet with Father to discuss it today." He did not seem to notice how, on one hand, he claimed to run the place, while on the other, he asked his father's thoughts.

"What does it entail?"

"I want the people of this wonderful city to build autonomous bots," Andrew said excitedly, wanting to hear his wife's opinion about his idea, but he was also aching to talk about the many possibilities of new technology. "Some years ago, Father developed plans for these autonomous creators. He has plans, drawings, and details. He has laid those to rest in his desk drawer. Now is the time for them."

"A-autonomous? Why on earth would you want to create and manufacture autonomous bots?"

"Yes. Teleos Autonomous Bots; they will be the very first in the entire region. Think about the toiling and effort each man has put into mining, for instance. The effort put into building this city. These bots will save on hard work in the future, giving our people an easier life. This is the life in which man will be able to lie back and rest in the shade of the palms while our bots work."

Amelia looked aghast, horrified!

"We have machines though, Andrew," Amelia interrupted with a rather low voice, sounding unsure of how great the idea was. "The machines do all the work."

No, they do not, Amelia. I hardly dare to call them machines at this time. These machines still require so much effort and energy to operate. For every machine, there are several men and women standing by—feeding, cutting, straightening, pushing, pulling, and cleaning.

"There is no end to the work for us created by these so-called machines. Yes, I agree they help, and we wouldn't have been able to achieve what we have without them, but we need to step up to the next level. These machines are in the past now. They belong in museums."

"What has brought this up? The men are not complaining, are they?" Amelia said, confused."

"Of course not, but I don't have to wait for my people to cry out before I recommend a solution that I believe will make life easier, do I? Did my father wait, or did he build a city?"

"Andrew—" Amelia started, but he cut her off.

"I really should be on my way now, darling." Andrew collected his papers together.

"I will be with you in no time," Amelia answered. "I shall come to assist you, as I always do when you need me. But if you expect me to back your intention to use the autonomous bots..."

"I will be expecting you," Andrew said, already close to the door before turning around and coming back again to give Amelia a peck on the cheek.

"I will see you soon," Andrew said, slamming the door behind him, making Amelia jump. Andrew had been a great husband, and she was glad their paths had crossed, but this was different.

He portrayed a lot of ease and quiet in accepting his new role, and Amelia had never realized the amount of work and commitment it took to run Teleos. But right now, she was sure Theodore was quite right and Andrew was developing notions 'beyond his station,' as Theodore put it.

On days like this, she would worry about his welfare and well-being. She did not know how to manage this. If she confided in Theodore something that Andrew had said in confidence, then she was being disloyal to her husband. A good wife would never engage in tittle-tat-tle.

But on the other hand, if she just let Andrew do his own thing and run amok with crazy new ideas—ones his knowledgeable father had already binned for one reason or another—then it would surely all go wrong, and the guilt and responsibility for that would be on her head.

Andrew was spending fewer hours at home and more in the office or with his father, discussing anything and everything to keep the city running smoothly.

He would eat less, sleep less, and talk less at home these days, and Amelia often caught him awake in the middle of the night, making plans and drafting ideas down on the scratchy parchment scrolls he always kept beside the bed for when ideas came into his head at night.

She could only hope he would truly discuss the autonomous bots with his wise father. But she feared what he might do if Theodore never gave his blessing for the development of the bots.

Once when the ideas came to fruition did Andrew clearly relax again, spend more time at home and even ask for vacations here and there. So, she knew to worry when he was this way because even the smallest idea could soon become everything, his obsession.

She now understood that, given some time, Andrew would usually accomplish his idea and return to being the wonderful husband she adored until the next idea entered his mind.

But this—the bots—felt different. Autonomous bot would never fall into the old ways and traditions and customs of his father had insisted he work to. Autonomous bots were not even something Theodore had wanted. Otherwise, the detailed plans and drawings would not still be languishing in his desk.

Leaving their own rooms that morning, there was just one thing on Andrew's mind. Autonomous bots.

He was determined to make it work some way and was ready to put in the work required.

Phillip stood a few meters away from the grand exit just as Andrew came out, approaching him with brisk steps. "Good morning, Master Andrew," Phillip said.

In Phillip's hands were sheaves of papers, likely ones he had prepared in accordance with his master's wishes the day before. Andrew noticed them, assuming they must contain work papers to sign, and more work to follow up on.

"Good morning. We'll go to my father's quarters and then the palace of gold before we leave for the factory," Andrew replied, walking smartly and holding his shoulders tall.

The resemblance between himself and his strong father was striking and unmistakable.

"Oh no, sir," Phillip jumped in, increasing his pace. "Master has asked to have the morning to himself."

"What do you mean?" Andrew slowed as he was already walking toward his father's quarters.

"They informed me this morning that he needed some quiet time and he asked to be left alone until the evening after we closed for the day," Phillip replied. "You should run everything, he said."

"And who passed this information across?"

"Michael, his right-hand man."

Andrew stood for a moment before continuing with his movement, heading the other way.

"Let us go straight to the factory, then."

Usually, Andrew would ask for updates on anything and everything happening in the factory and within the entirety of Teleos. When the day was over, Phillip would receive, and read the reports to Andrew. It was routine for Andrew to hear about it on the way to work, and he would then take the latest news and sit down over a second breakfast to discuss it with Theodore.

Now, that is denied to him on this day. He was oddly quiet as a result.

Arriving at the factory and with a concerned expression, Andrew spent just a few minutes looking down at the already active factory workers. There could not have been any worse day for his father to wish for time out. He needed to talk about autonomous bots.

Andrew needed to make these bots work. His people work too hard on things machines can handle. They barely have time for themselves!

Noticing a difference in Andrew's demeanor, Phillip interrupted. "Master Andrew, is anything the matter?"

The autonomous bots do not even have to be big. As long as they can help complete drilling, smelting, and processing of gold, and maybe even aid a little with silk processing.

"Sir?"

I do not have to give them any autonomous power. My father's drawings will have inbuilt mechanisms... safeguards. I could just give them as little as possible. Enough to just get by.

"Sir!"

Shaking his head, Andrew walked over and sank into his brown leather chair. "No. Just read me the report from the factory."

"Yes, master." Phillip put down the first sheaf of papers and brought out some others.

"Yesterday, we got word from Starlight that the chemicals used for dyeing would arrive two days later than usual because of some delay in production materials. Fiber production has been going very well for every other material except silk. The men have asked for some more time.

"Everything is working painfully slowly because of these delays, and when the chemical dyes eventually come, it will take the men a full two to three days to mix such a great quantity.

"The yarn department is on the right track, but after the next three sets of dyeing, we will be out of dye, but we expect Starlight to be delivered by then, so there shouldn't be any reason for production to stop."

"Are all department heads in this morning?"

"Let me see."

Phillip tapped on the tab before him to check the morning register. "All but Mr. Peter," he said. "He called in sick this morning. The stress on him from his workload has taken its toll."

"Hmm," Andrew replied.

"The security officers in Teleos reported zero crimes, no casualties on the roadways, and no cause for alarm or reinforcement in their department."

"That's not new, but it's always good to hear. Do we have any tourists in the city at this time?"

"Yes, the leaders of Cush and the Euphrates arrived in the early hours," Phillip replied.

"And my father has not met with them yet?" Andrew asked with a slight frown.

"No, he has not."

Andrew looked away from Phillip and turned to his own papers. Everything was running smoothly in the entire city and also in the factory. Well, almost everything. There were the delays to deliveries. There was the stress-related sickness.

There was the time it would take for the mixing of the dyes. Above all, he could not understand the fact that Mr. Peter had stayed off sick. He was one of the longest working staff in the textile factory and he led the dyeing department with great skill and resilience.

Andrew assumed he was falling sick due to the increase in first-hand interference with the dyes Teleos imported from Starlight. The intensity of the chemical had increased threefold because Teleos had also started producing textile for a big city on the outskirts, called Thulani.

Andrew had not assumed full duties as his father's second-in-command when Thulani had reached out to Teleos to become partners. I felt this major shift in the whole of Teleos despite how fulfilled the city was, since Thulani was home to the largest number of world-renowned fashion designers and icons, producing clothes and pieces that left people's jaws and eyes wide.

So, when they showed interest in the fabric produced in Teleos, even Theodore knew it would greatly increase revenue.

The day went by very quickly for Andrew as he stayed fixed on his screens, researching bots. He had rejected his usual late breakfast and barely asked for updates from the factory all morning. Being so focused on his current and anticipated plan.

"Can someone tell me where my husband has been taken to please?" Amelia said jokingly as she strolled casually into the mill, eyes fixed on Andrew.

Andrew looked up and smiled weakly at his wife.

He was tired but still mesmerized by her beauty every time he saw her.

"You're here already?"

"Already? It is past noon, and when you failed to check on me, I knew you would be knee deep in that research of yours." Amelia said, a little annoyed.

Andrew heaved a deep sigh.

"Well, what choices do I have?"

"Choices? Teleos is not dying, Andrew, nor in lack of anything that it needs," Amelia said, dropping herself into one couch positioned on the other side of Andrew's worktable.

"You need to focus and appreciate all that you have done so far for the people of Teleos. You are getting worked up again."

"Am I? I have barely even gotten tangible results from my research."

"I don't suppose you've had lunch today?"

"Not yet."

"A late breakfast?"

"The pancakes are still sitting fine in my stomach. I don't feel at all hungry, not even a little."

Amelia rolled her eyes. "I trust you met with Father to discuss your... ideas?"

He fell silent. She took it to be a no.

"Father did not wish to be disturbed today. Phillip told me that Michael had said..."

She heaved a great sigh of exasperation. She would try to distract Andrew with food.

"Phillip, would you be kind enough to call for the kitchen?" she said. "Ask for something substantial, for someone who has had nothing to eat all day."

Andrew laughed a little. "I had breakfast, Amelia. The most important meal of the day!"

"Please go ahead, Phillip," Amelia said softly.

"All right, Madam." Phillip headed out.

"So, what kept you away from me all day?" Amelia asked. "I sent a couple of messages to your inbox, but I got no response. I was becoming rather concerned."

"Hmm, I have been really occupied with work."

"Work?"

"Yes, work."

"Or your new idea? Which is it?"

"My new idea is work. Or at least, it will be a real work in no time. It will change Teleos for the better."

"I really think you do not have to worry about autonomous bots here in Teleos, Andrew. We have more important things to care about than technology and more pieces of machinery."

"Better things like what, exactly?"

"Like education, agriculture, healthcare. There are so many other things to do that the people would rather have than bots walking in their midst," Amelia replied, expecting a firm or immediate response from Andrew because he was not one to back down easily.

He looked down at the tablet in front of him.

After a few seconds of silence, he stood up and walked closer to Amelia.

"Darling," Andrew started and sat at the table right in front of Amelia, taking her right hand gently in his. "If we'd had autonomous bots when Mr. John Smith was alive, he would still be around and so would your mother. She only died from the grief of losing him."

Amelia swallowed hard and stayed quiet. It seemed like a mean comment, one that would hurt her.

And it had. He knew she would have nothing to say to that. It was true, but that still did not make it right for Andrew to race ahead with an idea Father would detest and deny.

He went on, "John Smith used machinery, yes, but there were casualties that would have been avoided if we had autonomous bots to do what he was doing. His death and many others would have been prevented if they'd been in place sooner. Can't you see what I'm trying to achieve?"

"I know that, Andrew," Amelia said under her breath.

"I want to make sure the people of Teleos are always safe, Amelia. We can give them healthcare too. I mean, even though he'd had good healthcare, he still did not make it. This means we really should spend more time preventing than curing, you know? Autonomous bots are a must."

"I know you're only trying to do the right thing, Andrew, and for the first time since yesterday, the idea does not sound so bad anymore," Amelia said with a weak smile.

"Thank you."

Andrew stood and walked to the window to look down at the factory, spending a few minutes simply watching the workers below.

"I am sorry if what I said about your father got you sad." Andrew said. He was still looking through the window but noticed Amelia was awfully quiet, making him feel bad about the manner in which he had spoken. More than that, he should never have mentioned her parents.

She had tears in her eyes.

"No, it's really fine," she said, not wanting to think about it any- more since it hurt too much.

Andrew turned around to see Amelia holding his tablet.

"I see you have done a lot of findings and research about these autonomous bots."

"Oh yes," Andrew said. "It just gets deeper and deeper with each new tab. It's remarkable what you can achieve with just a basic bot, but I intend to build one that's on another level."

"I can see that," Amelia said, still clicking away. "I think you forgot to hit the send button right here. Look."

Andrew leaned in to see what she meant. There was a message he'd composed but not sent.

"Tsk. I must have gotten carried away with something else," Andrew said, grabbing the tablet from Amelia and clicking send. "Enough of me. What have you been up to all day?"

"Me? I thought you would never ask," Amelia said, just as Phillip knocked lightly and opened the door. He walked in with a kitchen attendant following closely behind.

"I visited the clinic today," she said. "A patient I have been watching closely for some weeks now has shown signs of very significant recovery. She has been taking food and milk."

"Is that not beautiful?"

"Oh yes, it made me so happy that she is getting better. She's a young girl who works in one of the exotic eating houses downtown and I can only imagine what would have happened if the manager at the restaurant had not noticed her yellow eyes."

The kitchen assistant served Andrew's meal while Phillip stood by the door, hands folded in front of his chest.

"Now, think about this. What if we had autonomous bots that could scan for any health-related issues within the people of Teleos? Think about how beautiful that would be."

"Indeed. Many patients have been discharged, and a few more admitted for close monitoring, so I simply stayed around to give an extra hand at the clinic. I enjoy helping when I can."

"That's kind of you, Amelia," Andrew replied.

"All of these plans and notes I have already sent to you, Mr. Autonomous Bot." Amelia joked. After all, what could she now do but support her good husband and his ideas? It was clear he was going to develop these things with or without his father's help, and if Theodore did not want to talk...

Andrew sat on his chair and smiled a bit before putting his tablet down and digging into his food. Amelia remained standing, carefully eating the fruit salad the kitchen attendant had sent.

"Are there any rising issues here in the factory? Did any negative reports come?" she asked.

Andrew shook his head, still picking away at his food.

"And there are no reinforcements with any department at all? No repairs, all good?"

"All good," Andrew mumbled with food in his mouth. "The maintenance lead sure knows his job and does it well. That is why Father trusts him. You have probably seen for yourself, but Father has an amazing judgment of character. He seems to have this natural ability to know who is good and who he can trust. I guess that's one reason he's achieved all this."

"Then we should spend some time with him tonight." said amelia trying to get Andrew to talk to his father.She still hoped for Andrew to come to his senses and discuss the bot plans.

"Don't we always?"

"Yes, but we should spend more time this evening, for obvious reasons."

Andrew stared blankly and kept digging into his tomato pasta, the sauce dripping from the side of his mouth as he slurped each forkful. "What obvious reasons?"

"We should discuss your idea of producing a autonomous bot and get his view. I am sure you will be able to persuade him and he'll be delighted to invest his time in it. It should be easy enough to convince him, especially after you coaxed him to agree to build the golden mansion."

"I bet he would love to invest time in it," he agreed.

Andrew and Amelia enjoyed the rest of their meal in silence while Phillip attended to updates from different departments in the factory. They could hear workers from below cheering and making jokes at intervals and, for some reason, this made Andrew calm down a bit.

Amelia walked over to the window and saw some workers singing a song together in a happy way, even though they looked exhausted.

"Let's go join them," Amelia said suddenly.

"Huh?"

"The workers. Look, we should celebrate with them," she said again, packing up her things into her gold hand-knitted bag.

"You think so? We don't even know what they are celebrating. It may be personal."

"Even if it is personal, I'm sure they will be more than delighted to share." Amelia smiled excitedly, drawing Andrew to the idea, even if he wanted to do some more research.

The more of his time she could occupy, the better.

"Maybe we should head home immediately after," he said, suddenly surprising her. But then she realized he was joking at her expense. He knew exactly what she was up to.

She went along with the joke, still hopeful.

"I thought so too," Amelia agreed, delighted.

Andrew picked up his tablet and headed out with Amelia clinging to his arm.

"Uh-oh," Andrew said when they arrived at the floor where they had just seen and heard the workers singing. It was as if there had been a call or an emergency, each worker now dressed back in work garments and working away as they usually were.

"Guess we'll never know what it was they were celebrating after all," Amelia said, smiling at her husband. "But now that we're here, a walk around the factory would not be a bad idea, you know?" Amelia said again after a minute of silent walking. "We should see it up close rather than just from the view from the screen room."

She and Andrew setoff,walking down the clear hallway. Occasionally, a worker would pass by and perform a slight bow to Andrew and Amelia. Some simply smiled, and some waved, giving Andrew a sense of satisfaction and a feel-good factor about his day.

Chapter 5: A Dear Friend

"Umm, honey," Amelia said in a low tone. She stopped walking and pulled back at Andrew's arm. "I think I see someone I know from the past."

"Really? I thought your only friend left Teleos after she got married."

"Yes, I thought so too, but that person looks familiar." Amelia did not wait for a response from Andrew before releasing his hold and walking toward a lady down the hallway.

"Excuse me," Amelia said. The lady in question stayed still. She had an apron over her dress; it was stained with different dyes, so she must have been working in the printing department.

"Anna?" Amelia said, reaching forward. To her astonishment, the lady looked up, and it was just who she'd thought it was.

"Amelia!" Anna cried out and rushed in for a hug. "It's you! Look at you! How long has it been since I last saw you?"

"Yes, it's me, Anna," Amelia said. "Come here. It's been years since I saw you last, and it's so good to see you."

The two friends held each other tight for a few seconds and Andrew watched in admiration. Soon after they'd married, Amelia had shared that, like most, she had struggled with life after both her parents died within a short time of each other.

Losing one parent was traumatic enough, but to lose the second parent so soon after took its toll on her. She had taken a long time to grieve.

By the time she had partly recovered, all she cared about was work.

The only friend she'd ever had and who had stayed put was Anna.

"I thought you'd left Teleos! I thought I would never see you again!" Amelia cried out.

"Oh, Amelia! It is so good to see you again," Anna said. Her eyes had welled up a bit, and she kept them fixed on Amelia.

"It is good to see you too," Amelia said. "When did you move back to Teleos?"

"About three weeks ago," Anna said. "I am still trying to settle in. Whew!"

"I can imagine! So much has changed in Teleos," Amelia said with a gentle laugh. "So, three weeks and you are already working in the factory?"

"Ahem!" Andrew jumped in, clearing his throat to get some attention from the two ladies.

"Ah, forgive my manners," Amelia said, stretching out her hand toward Andrew. "Anna, meet my husband, Andrew. Andrew, meet my best friend, Anna."

Anna squinted a little and when she saw the badge on the breast pocket of Andrew's suit, she quickly took a bow. "Master Andrew," she said. "I'm privileged to meet you."

"Oh, please, no," Andrew said, smiling. "Not so formal."

He stretched his hand to shake Anna's. "We are family now."

Anna smiled sheepishly, wiped her hand on her apron, and took Andrew's hand in her own, still bowing as she received it.

"Come walk with us, Anna," Andrew said.

"But sir, I need to—"

"Nonsense, I'm sure your colleagues can manage for a while?" Andrew said to one of two men standing close by.

"Of course, sir."

"Thank you," Andrew replied with a smile, and they walked deeper into the factory. "So, what is work like for you here in the factory?" Andrew asked Anna. "Does it satisfy your needs?"

"Oh, it isn't bad at all." Anna spoke as though she were a shy person, but maybe that was partly due to walking and talking with the ruler of Teleos. "The work hours are very favorable, so they allow me some time to myself to help me settle back into life here in this great city."

"That's good," Amelia said. "I am so pleased you are enjoying your work and life here. A lot has changed since we last saw each other."

Amelia looked genuinely excited to see her friend.

"Oh my! We have so much catching up to do!"

Anna laughed a little. "I don't have a shift tonight; we can meet up somewhere later and talk. Does that work for you?" Anna suggested, looking at Amelia, then Andrew.

"Of course it does. I think the bread house has a special tonight; let's go there."

"Or maybe you could come over to our home?" Andrew jumped in. There was an enormous grin on his face as he looked at Amelia, then back at Anna with a subtle smile.

"Uh, I don't know if that's right... Me coming to your residence? I mean..." Anna mumbled her words. She had never been to the most beautiful home in the entirety of Teleos, but it was common knowledge how magnificent the house was.

"Oh, I have a meeting tonight, so I would not be present," Andrew said. "It will give you both time to catch up, and Amelia can show you around the home. I can understand your reluctance, but please don't turn down the offer because of who I am."

"Oh, Master. Thank you for asking. It's just a lot to take in. But I will accept with grace."

"It's my pleasure, and please call me Andrew."

"Oh... ok, Andrew, Master," Anna whispered, unable to let the title drop.

"Then that is sorted. It will be far easier for you both at home. As I said, I will be away attending a meeting, so you both can catch up while I am out."

"The *meeting* with Father?" Amelia asked.

"Yes, but it will be fine," Andrew said quickly when he noticed the frown on her face. "I am sure he will understand your absence when he hears you bumped into your long-lost friend here in Teleos. Besides, you do not have any interest in autonomous bot."

"Ha! Thank you," Amelia said. She leaned in and gave Andrew a peck on the check. "Please do send my regards and promise to update me when you get back."

But secretly, she would rather have been at the meeting, if only to ensure her husband really did discuss the autonomous bot plan. She had a feeling he might wriggle out of it and develop them.

"I will. Don't worry about work. Just make sure you have fun."

"Sure."

Andrew walked away ever so majestically, with Phillip following closely behind. In a few minutes of his voice echoing in the almost empty hallway, he was out of sight.

"Anna!" Amelia said, moving in to hug her friend again. "It is so good to see you."

"I am equally delighted. Anna said that she felt lonely when she moved into Teleos again. "I tried to find you, but everyone looked so different. It felt like the whole city had been wiped clean of everyone I knew! I felt so bereft, unable to locate my Amelia."

"I can imagine," Amelia said. "Many people from my neighborhood at Ashur have moved houses, and it gets so difficult to keep in touch with them."

"Ah," Anna said. "I can see that life has been very fair to you."

"What can I say?" Amelia said. "Anyway, are you done here for the day? This isn't the place for two friends who haven't seen one other for so long to have a catch up. And I'm sure you feel awkward chatting to me in front of so many others. If you're almost done, then we should move on. What do you say?"

"Umm," Anna pondered. "I'm due to finish at the next bell ring."

"That is close. So, you are done with your tasks, yes?"

"Yes, but the head of the printing press wants us newcomers around till the last sun, daily."

"Let's go. I will put in a word for you."

"But I won't get into... trouble, will I? Right, I forgot I was speaking with Mistress Teleos."

They both laughed and Anna took some time to get her things from the factory.

Soon, she was out, and they were on their way to the quarters.

Arriving at the magnificent property, Amelia gave Anna a *brief* tour of the house, promising to show her more when she visited next. Anna was awestruck by the sheer scale and detail of the place, the sheer grandeur and splendor of it all. Many had described it without even seeing it with their own eyes, but it was so much better than even they had guessed. And here was Anna, sitting with her friend—the wife of the leader of Teleos.

But tonight, they needed to discover what the other had been doing over these last few years. Finally, sitting in one of the many rooms, the conversation started.

It was not long before it led to the topic of marriage.

"It was not as delightful as I had imagined it to be," Anna said, now at ease with her surroundings. "I suppose he was like most at the start. He had been great for the first few months, but after some time, he just became very headstrong and extremely difficult to relate to."

"And nothing happened before then?" Amelia asked, concerned about her friend's experience.

"Well, I really can't say because I had a miscarriage around the time. He wanted to be a father so bad, and his mind was elsewhere. After we lost our baby, he threw himself into work."

"I am so sorry about this, Anna," Amelia said. She leaned forward and held her friend's hand. "If I had the slightest idea, I would have put in even more effort to check on you."

"You could not have known," Anna said. "The last time we spoke, it was still a paradise, and that was before we lost contact. But thanks for suggesting it."

"Yes, I remember that." Amelia poured herself some tea. "You are not drinking your tea. It's not Ceylon, don't worry."

Anna laughed and reached for the cup. "You remember. What is it?"

"It's oolong. Master Theodore processes its delivery himself," Amelia said. "A personal favorite. It's very good."

"Hmm," Anna said as she took a sip. "So exotic!"

"I told you!"

The two friends sipped tea quietly, staring straight out of the window as the sun began to set.

"So," Amelia continued. "How did you leave?"

"I didn't have to. He went to work one day and never returned. I thought something terrible had happened to him, so I was worried and tried to report to the police, but I got a message from him that was clear enough."

"Oh my."

"Yes. The rent expired the next month, bills were piling, and they turned off the water and coal, so I just had to leave."

"I'm so sorry about all of this, Anna," Amelia said. "Well, you're home now, and that is what matters. Plus, you have found your best friend once again."

"Yes. Oh, enough about me," Anna said. "Let us talk about you."

"There isn't much to say, honestly. Worked in the factory after my mom died, found a good man, and married him. Simple really."

"You make it sound as if it's nothing. But you are the luckiest lady in all of Teleos, married to the son of the great Master Theodore," Anna said, and kept sipping on her tea.

"Oh, please," Amelia said, feeling a little awkward. "Andrew is just as normal as any other man. He invited you here tonight. How many others in his position would do the same?"

"Yeah, right," Anna said with sarcasm. "You are correct, though. I doubt any other would have invited a relative stranger into the family home. Especially one on such a grand scale."

The two friends laughed and continued to catch up on all the years they had missed. Amelia showed Anna around more of the house and later, they had dinner together.

"I had a wonderful time here today, Amelia," Anna said with a smile. "But I really should get going now."

"Thank you for coming over, Anna. We still have a lot of catching up to do, but I am sure we have lots of time to do that."

"You bet!" Anna said. She stood, picked up her things, and headed toward the door.

"Anna," Amelia called out. "Sharon, packed this up for you."

"What?"

Sharon handed Amelia a basket almost filled to the brim. "Just some things for your house, some snacks to savor, and more oolong tea."

"You are far too kind," Anna said, taking the basket and admiring it for a few seconds. "Thank you so much, Amelia, and thank you, Sharon."

"Have a good night's rest, Anna. I will see you tomorrow."

"Thank you again and please thank your husband, too. I will see you tomorrow,night"

Anna departed in a flurry, leaving Amelia staring at the closed door. It had been almost seven years since she'd last heard from her friend, and she had missed her very much.

Anna had always stood with Amelia, especially when both of her parents died, and she'd done all she could to help financially, including helping Amelia get a job at the factory.

Initially, it had been Anna's job, but she was going to leave Teleos with her husband, so she put in a good word for Amelia with the head of her department.

As much as Amelia missed her friend and was so glad to have her around, she could tell something was just off. The manner with which she spoke and responded was unlike the cheerful and loving Anna that Amelia had known. It must have been the ordeal she had faced with her husband, which was enough for anyone to have become a shadow of themselves.

Anna had said she'd loved the man very much and had only imagined happily ever after with him, so the change coupled with the loss of her first pregnancy must have been a lot to take in.

"Please, clear the table, would you?" Amelia said to Sharon. "My husband will just take some fruits and that will be it."

"Yes, Madam." Sharon walked away into the kitchen with the teacups and came back with a napkin to wipe the dining table clean.

Time passed, and Amelia tried to take her mind off the matter with Anna.

She was thinking of the best way to help her, to make her feel love and care once more. Her mind became very clouded and worried, and she could not shake it off.

"Guess who is home?" Andrew said as he opened the front door that led straight into the living room.

"Hey!" Amelia exclaimed. She stood and gave him a quick hug. "That was quicker than I expected."

"It was?" Andrew asked, removing his jacket. "Thank you, Phillip, that is all for the night."

"Have a good night's rest, Mr. Andrew," Phillip said, taking a bow. "Madam Amelia."

"Thank you, Phillip," Andrew said.

Amelia nodded her head and watched the door shut.

"How did the meeting go with Father? Did you tell him about the autonomous bots? Did he approve?"

"Well," Andrew started. "Contrary to what we had expected, I did not get the chance to speak with Father tonight."

"Oh. Is everything okay?" Amelia asked.

"Yes, all is well. We had two leaders in the city for tourism and Father had not been available to meet with them since their arrival. They walked in just before I did, so that took priority, as you can imagine."

"Oh."

"After a series of reports and updates, I decided to retire and speak with Father at the dawn of tomorrow."

"Sounds just great."

"And what about you? How did your evening go with Anna?"

"Err, it was good, I think."

"Just good? You think?" Andrew asked. "When I left you in the factory, you both seemed overjoyed to have finally reunited."

Amelia chuckled. "It went well, just not as great as I thought it would."

"And why is that? Was it because I invited her here, do you think?"

"I am not sure. Just that something felt off about her, knowing that we used to be very best of friends before she moved away. She was not quite the same."

"I think you should give it some time and you both will catch on nicely. Maybe arrange to meet somewhere else the next time. Maybe go to the bread ovens, as you suggested."

"Hmm."

"At least you would not have to spend your days in the clinic or with Father, and back at home all the time," Andrew said, picking up a glass of water.

"Says the man who would spend hours with a tablet on one single research."

Amelia and Andrew continued to joke with each other for some time.

"Here, take these with you; we can enjoy them later in bed," Amelia said, handing the bowls of fruit to Andrew.

"These look fantastic," Andrew said, examining the fruit. "Thanks, Sharon," he shouted through to the kitchen.

They spent some time talking and enjoying the fruit, with Andrew mainly holding the conversation, talking about *his* autonomous bots soon after. Amelia nodded off, easily and quietly.

Andrew had been speaking to her about his research still, and she had kept responding until she simply went quiet. She did that all the time and would wake up the next morning, defending herself and saying she had not fallen asleep as quickly as Andrew suggested.

When Andrew noticed she had dozed off, he covered her with the thick wool blankets and walked to the window of their bedroom. The mansion where they lived with Master Theodore was right in the middle of the city, on a restricted floor on the top of the textile factory.

Because of this, it was such a beautiful sight to behold, especially at night.

My people. My responsibility. I owe them my energy and my zeal to make life easier and better for every single person in Teleos. This I will, I must.

Chapter 6: A Strange Meeting

Anna arrived home that night. She lived in a small single room in the city, about a fifteen-minute walk from the factory; it was a tiny space that she shared with a stranger who happened to need a housemate just as she moved into Teleos.

Anna felt so bad after the short meeting she had with Amelia the day before, and she could not overcome how bitter she felt.

She could not help but recall the times they had shared when they were younger.

After Amelia lost her father, her life had come crumbling down. The little money they'd had left after paying for the outstanding office bills. They had used to take care of her mother, who was then losing a lot of weight and being overtaken by grief.

She could not resume her job, and she kept Amelia at home too, because she was worried. Anna had been a strong pillar for Amelia and stood by her when all seemed to go south.

She had always been there to support Amelia and her mother, whether it was financially or just helping take care of her sick mother.

Anna was bitter at seeing how the tables had turned. Now, she was the one in complete need and her friend had the world to herself. Amelia had no worries whatsoever. In fact, visiting Amelia at her home had backfired, leaving her feeling resentful and filled with envy.

"Breathe. Take a deep breath, and focus on your breathing," she said to herself, trying to calm her mind, but it wasn't working.

"Are you sure everything is fine?" her housemate asked for the third time since she'd got home. "You do not look good."

"I'm fine," Anna replied sharply and went into her room where she tried to put things in a neat order to take her mind off what was troubling her. Then she recalled that Amelia had a maid who did all the chores, and she would never have to worry about putting rooms in order.

She remembered being served oolong tea, one of the most expensive in the region.

Then she looked at the basket Sharon packed for her. It looked as magnificent as could be.

Anna sat at the edge of her little bed, taking deep, sharp breaths. "I need to get out of here."

"Where are you off to? Is everything okay, Anna?" her roommate asked.

But Anna silently passed by the living room, fully dressed, and heading out of the house.

"I'm fine, really. I just need some air," Anna said, quickly shutting the door behind herself.

The streets were becoming quieter as night fell upon the city. The vast number of street lamps were giving brightness to the road, making the city look even prettier. Anna walked and walked without looking back, with no clear purpose, just wandering the city streets.

She was still new to the city, and apart from her daily commute to the factory, Anna had no idea where she was rushing to, but kept walking. She passed the well-lit factory, but Anna kept her head down, trying to erase any memories of her 'encounter' with Amelia.

Anna kept walking until she noticed a building in the distance with lights shining brighter than any in the city. This was intriguing. Well, at least investigating what that place was should give her something to do, something to divert her mind. Anna was interested in finding out what was in there. She had never noticed it before, but it certainly drew her attention.

Getting closer, Anna met with the most divine aroma filling the air, forcing her to stop and breathe in. Looking closely at the building, she could now make out it was made with bricks and had an awkward shape, unlike the rest of the buildings in Teleos.

In front of it, she could just make out what appeared to be an inscription, but could not read it from afar, so she walked closer. With each step she took, the fragrance increased in intensity, tempting Anna closer, as if it was drawing her into the building.

When she finally made it to the door, she looked above it, trying to make sense of the inscription. "Abad," Anna said loudly. "Abaddon, that's it. Abaddon. Hmm. Strange name."

Anna looked behind her, then stretched her hand to knock at the door, but as her fingers touched it, she found it unlocked. The door creaked open ever so slightly.

Looking behind her again, she took a deep breath. "What are you doing, girl?" she said.

But she slowly pushed against the creaking door, anyway.

"Hello?" Anna said, stepping over the threshold. "Hello? Is anyone here?"

The fragrant smell was now overpowering, and soft music played. Farther inside was a counter with smoke wafting up as though a meal was cooking.

"Is anyone here? I noticed the door open, so I came to check if everything was okay here?"

The lights in the building were brighter than any other she had seen before.

Yet oddly, they did not make her eyes hurt.

"Is anyone here?" Anna said again.

"Hello, Morana," a voice said, appearing to come from everywhere within the house, as though broadcast through a speaker. Anna looked around herself.

"Hello?"

A feminine figure walked out casually from another door in the room. She looked beautiful, her silky black hair falling over her shoulders in the most admirable way.

Her skin was shining under every light as she walked, and her gait was like that of a supermodel. "What brings you here?" the lady said. "Please, take a seat."

She gestured for Anna to sit on a long bench near the table, to which she agreed.

"N-nothing," Anna stuttered. "I was just passing by. I should be on my way now."

"No, something made you walk right in," the lady insisted. "I can tell."

Anna looked down at her feet as the lady took a seat opposite her.

The music in the room played on, but Anna could not make any sense of the lyrics.

"The lights," Anna finally said. "They shone brightly, and that attracted me. And then the inscription above the door."

"Then there is some darkness with which you need help. Am I correct?" the lady said.

She poured water into one of the glasses sitting on the table between them, then poured the other for herself. "Here, have some water."

"No, there isn't any darkness," Anna said. "I don't understand why you say that I need help."

"Morana, you need help," the lady said. "There is a darkness all around you. I know what I am talking about. I see it everywhere you go."

"Stop calling me that," Anna said. "My name is Anna, so please call me that."

"Hmm," the lady said. The contrast between her dark red nails and her silky black tresses was very distinct when she toyed with her hair.

"I was just taking a stroll to clear my head," Anna said, taking the glass and gulping down the water within it. She heaved a deep sigh and asked for another glass. "I am allowed to take a walk. It does not necessarily mean there is any kind of anything. No trouble, no darkness."

"You can talk to me," the lady said. "I should be able to help. You just need to tell me everything. Tell me what is troubling you. Tell me what this oppressive darkness is all about."

For the first few minutes, Anna was reluctant. She was not sure there was any need to validate what she had felt toward Amelia and the manner of luck that had fallen on each of their sides.

But after some convincing and comforting, she gave all the details about her feelings to her so-called new friend. Anna had supported Amelia throughout the worst time of her life, but here she was, married to the ruler of Teleos with all the privileges and benefits that went with it.

"You know what to do to overcome this feeling," the lady said gently, pouring the fourth round of water into Anna's glass.

"I do?" Anna said, rather confused. Oddly, she felt slightly better after pouring her heart out to this lady, getting things off her chest.

"Of course," the lady said. "You have the power to make all things right."

"I still don't believe I do. I just work in a factory. I'm just a nobody in this great city."

"You will see. Now, be on your way and everything will fall into place. The darkness will lift soon enough. You just need to give it time. That is all."

After a few more minutes, Anna walked out through the front door and headed home and thankfully, her housemate had gone to bed already, so she would avoid any further questioning.

Anna slept soundly, completely over all the hatred and bitterness she had felt some hours ago, but also completely oblivious of all that had happened in the bright building she had just visited.

It was odd, as though nothing at all had come to pass, as if she had not been anywhere.

Chapter 7: A Possession

Nothing could have prepared anyone for the thunderstorm that greeted Teleos the next morning. Like most cities, they had experienced storms in the past, but this was on another level. Many routes were closed due to the rising water levels, and a vast number of rooftops had been brought down by the ferocious storm. In the past, any such change in the weather, especially one as fierce as this, had always been broadcast so that everyone could prepare.

This storm, however, was unexpected, catching the whole city of Teleos off guard and causing mayhem and destruction within the city and beyond. People started from the windows hoping to see a break forming in the weather system, but nothing changed. The city was covered by this vast cloud.

Aloud rumble made Amelia jump from her sleep and she looked out the window to see the rain battering against it, obstructing her view of the city.

Andrew was not beside Amelia when she woke up, and neither was he in the bathroom. Using the back of her hand to wipe her eyes awake, Amelia was now searching all over the rooms for him. Where could Andrew be? The dark clouds from the rain had made it seem like it was still the early hours of dawn. But it was not. It was at least mid-morning and she had overslept, having been woken so many times.

"Andrew?" Amelia called out, her voice hoarse. "Andrew? Are you here?"

There was no answer.

He might have left for his daily work, but he would never leave without letting her know. Grabbing the robe from the couch, she walked out of the bedroom in search of her husband.

"Sharon?" Amelia said quietly, almost in a whisper. She cleaned her eyes again as she walked through the hallway that separated her bedroom from the living room. The rains became more violent, and Amelia could hear the crackling sound of lightning gathering.

"Yes, they could easily be of help." Amelia heard a familiar voice coming from Andrew's study. Entering, it surprised her to see Anna there.

"Oh, what a wonderful surprise to see my friend and my dear husband both awaiting me!" Amelia said. Anna stood and walked forward to hug Amelia. "Good morning. Did you rest well?"

Anna, of course, had not rested well, but this was due to how unsettled she had been.

"Definitely a great surprise seeing you here so early, but a pleasant one too," Amelia replied, returning Anna's hug. Anna was feeling better about everything now, no longer resentful.

It was still a strange phenomenon how she had met with the odd woman and all her ill feelings had waned as if they had been mere specks of dust carried by a strong wind.

Of course, she would still have liked all these riches and this life for herself. But things were as they were, and it was hardly dear Amelia's fault that their fortunes had turned out as they did.

"You are welcome," Anna said with a chuckle.

"Your smart friend saw the clouds gathering and thought it'd be nice to have tea with us," Andrew said. "She arrived just before the storms hit."

"I'm glad you didn't get stuck," Amelia said. "Any later, and I don't think you would have made it here."

"Darling," Andrew said, kissing his wife. "Anna was just saying she worked with an engineering firm back where she used to live and they tried building an autonomous bot a couple of times," Andrew said. "What a coincidence, don't you think? I was not even aware that anyone except my father knew about autonomous bots. It is a marvelous thing that you brought Anna into our life."

He looked delighted.

He had met someone who had been involved with manufacturing his dream.

"Ah!"

Amelia looked way less delighted. autonomous bot? Anna? How?

"Yes," Anna blurted. "They tried and failed a couple of times, but right before I left, there was a scheduled meeting with another firm with a high success rate in manufacturing autonomous bots."

"Just in time for us to find answers!" Andrew clapped his hands together in excitement.

"Yes," Amelia said, her voice trailing off a little. "An engineering firm. Hmm. Well, you kept that quiet, Anna. What else are you not telling your best friend? You know, correct me if I am wrong, but I could have sworn you said you worked in a bakery for most of your time in Justicia, did you not? I don't remember a thing about an engineering firm. I mean, are there even such firms? Andrew, have you heard of any? I could also have sworn that you found your father's plans for autonomous bots unusually innovative. Did you not say so yourself?"

"The autonomous bots... the engineering works," said Anna, trying to think up answers to the questions that had come toward her from Amelia. "Oh, I must have missed mentioning it in all the new excitement of being reunited with my friend," Anna said. "The bakery, yes... I was a baker's hand for a long time, but the engineering firm was set up by, umm, someone I met."

Well, that explained it all, then. Except that it didn't.

The talk of autonomous bots was quite preposterous. It was as if the two of them were under some kind of influence or spell. Had they been drinking something? Partaking of an herbal concoction?

"Oh," Amelia said, shaking off the suspicious thoughts running through her mind, smiling.

She had to always smile when Andrew was around. Marital friction was not acceptable, particularly not if it was the wife who started the argument. She should support her husband.

"That really would be marvelous for the project if we could get in touch with this company."

"Yes, I have given her a few details on what I aim to achieve, and she says it is more than possible—" Andrew said. "Anna knows so much. I am so thrilled we crossed paths."

Thrilled indeed, said the blank look on Amelia's face. *autonomous bots this, autonomous bots that. Well, just wait till Theodore hears all about this. It's quite ridiculous. He shall put a stop to it, I'm sure.*

"Autonomous bots can do lots of things," Anna jumped in again. "In some cities far from here, autonomous bots treat people for their ailments and take orders from the hungry, awaiting their food from the bakery or laundry, or the cookhouse. It is almost the barest minimum to want autonomous bots to drill for gold and help in the factory as Andrew intends."

"This is such great news! What steps do we need to take next?" Amelia said, trying to seem supportive while Inside, her blood was boiling. She was seething.

Now, she sorely regret bringing Anna here. The woman was nothing but trouble.

"Andrew said he sent a quote request to one of the largest engineering firms in the region," Anna replied. "I sent a message to my previous employer and maybe we can compare before we know who to work with? At least we'll have some inside knowledge to work with."

"Did you hear that?" Andrew said excitedly. "Weeks of worries are all gone in just one discussion. I'm so glad you two bumped into each other."

Amelia laughed lightly and rubbed her arms. "I'm so glad this is happening."

But her lips were down-turned in a crooked grimace.

The two were so excited, however, they did not even notice Amelia's offense

"And I am so glad to be of help!" Anna said, taking the glass of water resting on the side table close to her and taking a sip.

"Ah, the sun is almost setting," Anna said. "It's easy to forget that I am still an employee in the factory. Thank you for another warm welcome, and I'm glad I could be of help to your future project, Andrew. I need to head off to work now."

"If we didn't have to meet my father in the next hour, we would have excused you from work today," Andrew said. "But please, we would be glad to have you around any day, any time."

Amelia's expression brightened. They were set to meet his father. Then the day was improving at last. Well, thanks to all the gods for that!

"Most definitely, Anna," Amelia said, her gut churning.

"Thank you so much," Anna replied. She stood and proceeded toward the door. "I enjoyed every moment with you." She directed the comment toward Andrew. This only made Amelia's ire boil all the more. Oh, she hated that damn woman now! Thank goodness she's gone!

Standing just outside the study, Sharon led Anna out of the mansion.

"That was quick," Amelia said when Anna left the room. "Very quick indeed."

"Huh? What was quick, my dear?"

"You! You both bonded very quickly. How long has she been here?"

"Not too long. But she is such a pleasant person, and I can hardly wait for all my plans to work out. She has been such a help. I cannot possibly describe how much. She's a delight!"

"Yes, I am glad too," Amelia said. "We get to see Father this morning, yes?"

"Yes, we do," Andrew replied. "We should be on our way before the moon shows itself."

"Good, then why do we not depart right now?"

"You seem eager to see him? Even more so than usual."

"Not really, but it's always good to see Father, especially to get his thoughts on the autonomous bots."

"Yes, I'm looking forward to talking to him and explaining that we now have some more information from someone involved in their manufacture."

"It will be good to see what he says. Anyway, I need to bathe and prepare for the meeting. I just hope this weather calms. It seems to be getting worse."

Andrew was adjusting his hair when there was a knock on the door.

"Good morning," Phillip said, entering the quarters.

"Good morning to you too, Phillip," Andrew said. "I hope father has not asked for alone time again."

"No sir," Phillip said, chuckling. "He cleared up his morning to see you. Juggled a few things around, so you have his full attention."

"Finally!" Andrew said. "Let's do it. Darling, are you ready?"

"Yes, I'm coming." They left the house, and Phillip shut the door behind them.

"Look," Andrew said to Phillip as they took the long hallway above the factory. "Starlight delivered the scrolls already? "

"Yes, sir," Phillip said. "It's in the parchments. I updated it this morning."

"Is there anything else I should know before meeting with Father?" Andrew said, stopping in front of the next door that led into his father's quarters.

"Nothing distinct, sir."

"Good. As soon as we get into the meeting, send out word that no one interacts with the dyes till I say so."

"Yes, Mr. Andrew. You can depend on me."

Andrew opened the door, revealing the extravagant room where Theodore held guests. Amelia had seen it a lot of times but was still astounded every time she saw it.

"My son!" Theodore said from the end of the hall. He stood from his large, bejeweled chair and walked toward them to give each a tight hug. "I have missed you very much."

"Oh, you have no idea, Father," Andrew said. He held onto the hug for longer before finally releasing his father and giving him a peck on both cheeks.

"My daughter," Theodore said.

"Father, it is good to see you."

"I feel very happy too!" Theodore said. "Both of you, please come. There is so much catching up to do. I do apologize for not seeing you sooner—unexpected guests."

"Yes, Father, there is so much to discuss, and there's a huge icing on the cake too!" Andrew said. The excitement in his voice was almost palpable.

"Icing? Cake? What cake?"

Then he suddenly realized what his son meant. "Ah, you mean you're up to something, eh?" Theodore asked. "I can hardly wait to hear."

Theodore ordered grape juice and asked for the table to be set for breakfast.

"I assume you knew better than to have breakfast at your house."

"Andrew laughed. "We always look forward to eating here with you."

"Great!" Theodore said. "Let me tell you something. I have been on my own for some time now, taking some time to reflect and retrace my steps. I ask you both to take note of what I am saying. It's so important. You must learn to do this over time, so the enemy does not creep in on you. Always question things and never act on impulse. Think things over before committing."

"And remember what I have said: always stick to the old ways and materials."

Andrew's face was the picture of misery.

"Yes, Father."

They served the blood of the grapes while two staff set the table.

"So, let us get down to it," Theodore said.

"Thank you, Father," Andrew said, adjusting himself on his seat. His hands were shaking in view of what his father had just said yet again. It was as if his father had a sixth sense.

Andrew ordered Phillip to hand him the first documents from the bundle of scrolls.

Then he spread the first on the table, careful to cover the body of it with his large flat hand.

"Father. What I have in my hand is my plan for the most brilliant idea to move Teleos ahead—and I know you have just spoken to me about taking my time and working in the old ways, but what I feel is—"

"Ah!" Theodore raised his hand, signaling for Andrew to stop. "Now, now, Andrew, please stop there. Surely you understand by now that the most important thing is to inform me how our people are. So, please tell me about my people first."

Andrew cleared his throat as his hand fell back. He flipped the parchment scroll upside down and weighed it with a large heavy goblet of clay, so nothing showed through from the other side.

"Yes, sorry, Father. Everything is going well," Andrew said. "Now, if I may tell you about—"

He looked around himself, feeling rather ashamed and afraid. His voice shook too.

"Everything is going well?" Theodore asked with a frown, his voice in a high pitch. "That is such a vague report, Son. Everything is going well? When did I ever teach you this?

"Did I not just labor to explain how you must take things slowly, how you must be calm about them, and never rush? Then why do I get the distinct feeling that you cannot wait for me to shut up about the people and their welfare so that you may launch into a tirade about how you want to rush into something? Something of the very kind against which I have warned you."

"Th-the factory is running fine, and the workers are g-good too," Andrew replied.

"Father, the clinic does not lack any resources. The young lady with the liver disease is recovering very quickly and those who are ill are responding quickly to treatment," Amelia jumped in, trying to save her husband from Theodore's wrath. Even though she was sorely hurt by Andrew's secret liaison with the awful Anna, and even though she loathed the mention of those infernal autonomous bots, she did not want him to get into deep trouble.

Theodore sat back and put his hands together over his mouth.

"I hear Mr. Peter is unwell," Theodore said. "Have you found out what happened to him yet?"

Andrew remained quiet, shifting in his seat because he was getting uncomfortable.

"Andrew, do you know what happened to Mr. Peter? Do you know the reason he is so ill? Have you even seen him yet?"

"No, Father," Andrew replied in a whisper.

"Listen," Theodore said. "And this goes for you too, Amelia. When I handed this city to you, Andrew, I gave you very clear instructions to let you know that the people of Teleos are as important as Teleos itself. Do you remember me saying this to you?"

"Yes, Father."

"And that they need your undivided attention," Theodore said.

"Yes, Father, but—"

"No buts, Andrew. They are *your* full responsibility, and *your* duties exceed just listening to reports from your right-hand man."

Andrew looked at his father, then at Phillip, who stood in a corner.

"There is always work to be done. It's not just about new projects. The people come first."

"But Father, I was thinking about the autonomous bots—"

"autonomous bots are not important at this time!" Theodore said at the top of his voice and Andrew stayed quiet. He could not remember the last time he had seen his father so full of rage.

"If you do not take care of the seemingly small things that you have been given," Theodore said after a long stretch of very uncomfortable silence, "then how do I have the confidence to bless you with some more? You were doing well, Son. But this is unacceptable."

"Father," Amelia jumped in. "We have failed, and we will retrace our steps. Please forgive us. We will take note of our failures and promise it will never happen again."

"Forgive us, Father," Andrew said unwillingly. He had a slight frown on his face, and he did not maintain eye contact with Theodore.

"I do not have a hard heart toward my children," Theodore said. "But I do not wish to be interrupted from rest knowing that my city is not in safe hands. Cush has not received farming supplies in the past two weeks, and they thought we had an unsettled dispute with them.

"Their ruler came to visit along with that of the Euphrates to appeal to me a break in a relationship that I had not the slightest idea about. So, while you were researching these so-called *autonomous bots,* there were potentially damaging events happening under our noses."

Andrew's world came crashing down. He had spent his weeks researching, and it had gotten even worse when the idea seemed to be the turnaround point for Teleos, all in the wrong way.

"I will fix this, Father."

"You should, otherwise..."

Otherwise what? the expression on Andrew's face said.

Theodore stood and walked toward the dining room. "Come, let us eat."

Andrew grabbed Amelia's hand, and they walked to the dining room, following Theodore.

"So, tell me about this new idea of yours, Son," Theodore said at last.

Andrew's eyes lit up immediately. He sat to Theodore's right while Amelia helped with serving everyone's meal from the main dish.

"Yes, Father," Andrew said, signaling for Phillip to bring the briefcase to him. "I figured that here in Teleos, we have a lot of resources. Thanks to your wisdom and kindness, we will not run out of our resources even after many years of inactivity. However, I thought it would be a major deal-breaker if we could build our own autonomous bots. Following in your great tradition of technology."

He thought that flattering his father might work. Or that it could help, anyway.

"Hmm."

"I think they would help reduce the hazards that occur in the city."

"Hmm."

"I think they will make us more productive and safer. More cost-effective and—"

"Are you thinking of the city or the factory?"

"The factory. I mean, the city," Andrew corrected. "The entire city. *And* the factory. Both."

"I don't see how autonomous bots would help the city, Andrew."

"Father—"

"Do not be disheartened. It is not a bad idea, Andrew. Not overall."

"It is not?"

"No, it is not. That is why I sat and sketched them out at that time, many moons ago."

Andrew's face brightened, and he sat up straighter. "So, Father. I could just—"

"*No,*" said Theodore, emphatic. "You cannot *just* do anything. Autonomous bots are not what we need in Teleos right now, son." Theodore said, leaning in and tapping Andrew on the shoulder. "We have no need for a new technology of that sort."

Andrew was perplexed. How could his father say this? It was obvious to him and to everyone that Theodore had spent much of his rule selectively introducing that very thing!

What was wrong with his father that he would pretend he had never done so?

But there was no point in arguing. Even if Andrew was supposed to be the ruler of Teleos now, there was no sense at all in asserting what he believed were his rights.

There was no point in fighting, either. Even if Theodore had always told him in no uncertain terms that he must stand up for what he believed in!

He was quietly simmering. No, boiling. Writhing and flailing in his own skin.

Sometimes, poor Andrew hated being the ruler who was not allowed to rule.

"All right, Father," Andrew said. "I believe you are correct. You are always correct."

He was still seething. One day... one day, he would get to do his own thing.

One day, he would make his own decision and not consult about it. One day.

He sighed, and his mouth turned down. The food was no longer tasty, and the blood of grapes suddenly seemed sour, leaving a nasty residue in his mouth.

The beautiful lute music sounded like a posse of male cats screeching into the night.

And as for those wall hangings and tapestries featuring nubile women, they were irksome.

They continued eating quietly while Theodore gave random reports of what the leaders of Cush and the Euphrates had come to discuss.

"We enjoyed every bit of this with you, Father," Amelia said when breakfast was over and they were about to leave. She had still noticed Andrew was a bit quiet during the entire meeting.

She wanted to sound as neutral as possible, and it was always good to give thanks for the food. She edged towards her husband and gave him a sharp dig in his ribs. He flinched.

"What was that for?" he whispered, his face a picture of annoyance at his dear wife.

"You know!" she whispered back.

"I don't know," he whined, now sounding like a little boy.

"Give thanks for the food!" Her own expression was one of fire and flame. Sometimes, she could barely believe she had chosen to marry such an obstinate, self-indulgent man.

"I enjoyed it too," Theodore said in the most miserable tone. He still did not thank his father.

Theodore walked them to the door before tapping Andrew's shoulder again. "Son, I love and respect you very much. I trust you know this and do not let pigheadedness guide you."

Well, that did not help much, though it was good for any son to hear his father loved him.

"I know that, Father," Andrew replied, looking directly at his father this time. He gave his father a cold, unmoved stare. It seemed as if the atmosphere had grown icy between them.

"Then you must know that I have your best interests at heart."

"I know that too."

Another unsmiling grimace came. "Father, I need to go. I have things to do, people to see. Just as you said, I must."

"Very well. Then have a good day today," Theodore said. "And check on Mr. Peter, will you?"

That rubbed salt into Andrew's already open wound. Must his father micro-manage everything? Even the things they had already discussed and decided upon?

If so, then what was the sense in him appointing his son as the ruler in Teleos?

"I will let you know as soon as I find out anything. I shall go there right away."

Phillip held the door open for them to pass.

Amelia was already out when Theodore called out again.

"Andrew! You must stay focused on the work that involves the people and the city of Teleos. Do not allow the enemy to creep in on you while you are asleep. Please remember that. And remain working with the old ways, as I have said many times. Forget about autonomous bots. Forget technology."

"Yes, Father, I shall stay vigilant," Andrew replied. "And I will work only in the old ways."

"Please, stay vigilant," Theodore replied with a lot of emotion in his voice. The door shut behind them almost immediately, and Theodore was left by himself with his thoughts.

He was a little bothered and he could not hide it. The idea his son had put forward was not a bad one, but it was ambitious and was sure to bring about even more great distractions.

Theodore's main concern was that his son appeared to be totally immersed in the idea of building these autonomous bots, even to the point of failing to provide sufficient updates on the people and events within Teleos. Andrew had never failed to deliver a concise explanation of how the city was faring along with the well-being of these great people. In short, Andrew liked lofty ideas.

Andrew liked to get carried away on big projects that reaped the little rewards for the people.

People who, over the years, had built what his son was now controlling.

Andrew had been proposing something which, in fact, would have harmed the people by taking away their hard-earned jobs, damaging their wealth and their self-esteem.

Not only that, but he also felt certain that if the good Amelia was not around to keep his wayward son on the straight and narrow path, Andrew might already have run with the idea.

It was just like the golden mansion. Yes, he had let his son develop it and build it with a view to keeping the gold of Teleos safe and out of the hands of thieves. It was a nice idea.

But no longer could Theodore wander the city and hand out nuggets of gold or small coins to the poor. Now, when the poor required something, or if Teleos needed to purchase something, it was as if their hands were strapped behind their backs! They had no coins anymore. No gold.

What was the purpose of staring at a mansion of gold when none of it was available to use?

This boy of his had grand ideas that came from somewhere other than his brain. He did not use his intellect for the good of the people! Instead, he let the poor go hungry.

He was letting all the workers who had built this fine city struggle and toil.

Something wasn't right, and Theodore sensed repulsion in the conversation with his son.

"Michael," Theodore called out loudly.

"Yes, Master," Michael replied, walking from the corner of the room to meet Theodore.

"Michael, I need reports on what is happening in the city. On everything. Hide nothing from me, do you hear? I need to know what the boy is doing with every second of his time."

"Sir," Michael replied. "May I get this from your son, Andrew?"

"No, get the information yourself from the heads of every single department in the factory and every single department within the city. I want a different perspective, and I trust you implicitly to deliver. Also, Andrew and Amelia must not know about this. Do you understand?"

Michael shifted his stance before speaking again.

"Of course, Master. Is there anything I should be made aware of? Anything, in particular, I should be looking for?"

"No, Michael. Just gather the information from each department like you used to do when I was running the city."

"Yes, Master. My only concern is that every department now reports directly to your son, and it may be difficult to receive information from them. They may refuse to give it to me."

"And that is why I am sending you, Michael. You are still my chief right-hand man," Theodore said. "They shall not refuse. I sense they will welcome it with open arms if my instincts are correct that Andrew's attention has been going in all the wrong directions. It appears my city and my people still need me, but I need to know how I can be of assistance."

Michael nodded and wrote this request on his scroll.

"Would that be all, Master?"

"Yes, Michael. Try not to draw too much attention to the fact. Just treat it as you would have back in the day. The day when we worked alone together and when everything was smooth."

Chapter 8: The Informant

Amelia had followed Andrew straight to the office that morning and they had a heartfelt conversation about what Theodore had said. They had only just rounded up and spent a few minutes with reports when Anna knocked lightly on the door.

"Hi, Anna," Amelia said when she saw Anna standing at the door. "I didn't expect to see you so soon." Amelia was surprised to see her again, barely six hours since she'd been at the house.

She also wondered why Phillip did not inform them of her presence before letting her in.

Andrew looked up from his tablet and smiled widely when he saw Anna.

"Anna, so good to see you," Andrew said, closing the open tabs on his tablet and looking up at Anna. "Please, take a seat. Oh, my…" He grinned ear to ear. "You are my ally, my friend!"

He was speaking about her fondness for the autonomous bot idea, of course. Amelia bristled.

"Thank you," Anna said. She found an empty couch opposite of Amelia and sat quietly. "I didn't realize this office overlooked the entire factory. And you have all these screens too. I never believed it to be true, and here I am, watching my own workstation sitting empty."

"Oh really? Why did you disbelieve that it was so?"

"I thought the heads of departments only said that to get us to work faster and more diligently," Anna said.

Andrew laughed loudly at this. "Oh, we can see all that happens from up here, as you can see. It's a good thing to be able to monitor each department and have to have communication with each section. If I need anything, I simply speak into this and relay my message to whoever," Andrew explained, holding the intercom. "The wonder of technology!"

"Hmm. I suppose so."

Anna looked around for a minute or two, avoided Amelia's gaze completely, and then went on to talk to Andrew.

"During my free time earlier, I sent inquiries to three other engineering firms, my last employer worked with, and now all four have sent in their quotes. I know they're only quotes, but you can see the difference from each company."

"Brilliant!" Andrew exclaimed. "That is very brilliant, don't you think so Anna?"

Amelia shot him a confused look, wondering why he was still intrigued by this despite the long talk they'd had just before Anna walked in. The autonomous bots were never going to happen!

"Can I see them?" Andrew asked.

He was too excited to even take notice of his wife or the way she glared at him.

"Of course," Anna said. She clicked away on the small tablet in her hand before handing it over to Andrew. "Here it is. They're in no particular order. Just swipe right for the others."

Standing, Andrew rushed to take the tablet. He swiped and the look on his face showed how impressed he was by what he saw.

"This is amazing, Anna!" Andrew said. "Even the costliest quote here is lower than the one I got! I'm so grateful for you obtaining these, Anna."

"Well, I contacted old friends. We trade with one another in the old way. I get the best deals."

"See, Amelia!" he cried out. "This is what Father does not see. By using the old ways together with new technology, we get the best of both worlds!"

Amelia looked disgruntled. "Your father wants only the best of *this* world, dear," she voiced.

"That is so kind of you," Andrew said again to Anna, wholly ignoring his wife's views and tone. "Getting a sample or two of these smart autonomous bots for Teleos would go unnoticed in the revenue, and we would not need it to pass through any procedures or tests for confirmation.

"They have been put through rigorous testing already, so we have no need to carry out a testing program ourselves. Think about it. We can use them straight away. And in just the same way my father came around to see my vision when I married you, Amelia, or when I proposed the idea for our golden mansion, he will thank me in the end. I know he will."

"Hmm—" Amelia said. "I think you should be more cautious, darling. You know how Father feels about rushing into things. You also know his opinion on autonomous bots. And do not forget—"

He was not listening.

Meanwhile, Amelia was worrying about poor Mr. Peter.

Andrew had promised to call on him and they still had done no such thing.

The moment Andrew was away from his father, he had fallen right back into his old ways of plotting and planning their technological revolution.

"I have just sent all quotes to your tablet," Anna interrupted. "Including the details of the contact person for each firm, if that would help?"

"Most definitely," Andrew said, reaching for his tablet and clicking away.

Amelia looked at Anna, trying to fathom out why she was at work so early, adding to her suspicion from earlier when Anna had just appeared at their home.

There was something unusual about her, but Amelia could not make it out. Many years ago, when they had been closer, Anna loved early morning adventures, so it was not a complete surprise to see her at her house so early that morning. But something still wasn't sitting right.

"Sweetie, can I have a word?" Amelia said, but Andrew did not respond. It was almost as if he did not hear.

"Andrew?"

"Hmm?" He looked up in a hurry and stared blankly at his wife.

"Can I have a quick word with you outside?"

"Oh, I was just about to leave," Anna said with a smile. "I cleared my schedule down at the factory for a few minutes, so I guess that is over."

"Oh…" Andrew said, now shifting his attention back to the tablet in his hand. "We should meet up sometime to discuss this further. This is great work, Anna. I can't thank you enough."

"Of course," Anna said. "Amelia will let me know when you are free, and we can schedule something."

"Thank you."

"See you soon," Anna said, heading out. "Goodbye, Amelia."

"Bye."

Amelia sat up straight in her chair. Andrew took no notice of his environment, or of how much time was passing.

"You don't think that we should listen to Father?" Amelia asked.

"What?"

"Father's instruction, Andrew," Amelia replied, a little exasperated. "It was just some hours ago when we were with him, and he said to ignore this idea completely. You have always listened to him, and he is always right in what he says. Why is this so different?"

"Amelia," Andrew started.

"You are disobeying Father's instructions," Amelia said, frowning. "Outright disobedience."

"No! Listen to me, please. *I* run Teleos now. He is just being stubborn."

Amelia stared back at him and crossed her hand in front of her chest as he walked closer.

"Father disagrees with this idea, not because he thinks it is bad," Andrew said. "But because he fears that the people will not need his governance anymore. He has to meddle in everything."

"Andrew, what are you trying to say?"

"Just listen to me. These autonomous bots, contrary to what Father thinks, will help Teleos climb up the ladder of importance in the region. Every single city around will throw in their workers and resources so we could build for them too. Then we leverage that and keep them under us, needing us. This is real value, Amelia. Can you not see it?"

No, she could not see it. What she *could* see was an unholy mess developing.

"I just don't think we should be going against Father's will," Amelia said.

"We are not doing that, Amelia," Andrew defended. "We are simply thinking faster and farther than he is, and in the end, he will be glad we did. This is a chance to show him I can do things alone. There will come a time when he will not be able to make these decisions, and this opportunity will show him I can lead Teleos forward."

Amelia sighed and dropped her hands. There was no point in saying anything. Father was right. Andrew was rushing ahead with nonsensical plans, ignoring the real needs of the city.

And ignoring what the people required. People such as Mr. Peter.

"Can you please trust me on this one?"

"I'm trying to, but you saw how angry Father was yesterday."

"Thank you. I will not let either of you down."

For some reason, he seemed to have taken it, that she had backed down.

Now, she found herself stuck, since a wife must not argue with a husband. Once a husband had reached a decision, that was that. She loved him despite his stubborn ways.

Andrew returned to his brown chair, admiring the documents Anna had sent to him via the new technology, the existence of which his stubborn old mule of a father was now denying!

"So, we just keep this away from him completely?" Amelia said.

"Yes, we do. We would not have to hide it for long, especially now that we have this additional inside information from Anna."

"Hmm, alright," Amelia said. "But I don't feel comfortable going against Father's word."

"Trust me, darling. There will be a time when we cannot ask for Father's advice. So, just think of this as that time. I mean, what could go wrong?"

Andrew spent even more time with his tablet, barely taking notice of Amelia. She tried to keep busy too, but she could not help but be worried about what they were planning to do.

She paced around the room, watching time pass slowly. When lunch came, Andrew refused to eat until it became too stale.

"Honey, we should go to see Mr. Peter before visitation is close for the day," Amelia said. "Father will no doubt ask you for an update on his health."

She had gotten tired of sitting around in the office doing nothing and even this was unusual because there was always something to do.

Sighing, Andrew lowered his tablet.

"You think you can do that for us, please?"

"Father says he needs *us* to find out how he is recovering," Amelia said. "*We* should do that, don't you think? This wouldn't have been an issue before. So, why now? *We* need to go."

"I am occupied, head deep in this," Andrew replied. "Luckily, these companies are just as interested in working with us and the responses are immediate and quite detailed. If you could send my warm greetings to Mr. Peter, I am sure it would be enough."

Amelia smiled a fake smile and picked up her bag.

"I will be back soon," Amelia said. "Try to eat something."

"Yes, all right. Please tell Phillip to come in."

"All right."

Amelia walked out of the office with a mix of emotions. She was both scared and worried for Andrew. The last time he had been like this was months back, a few weeks into their marriage.

An issue had just come up with an invading city, Golgotha. Even though Theodore was present, Andrew had gotten himself so worked up that it felt almost impossible to appeal to him.

As she walked to the clinic, she prayed silently for this phase to be over. For the first time, she was glad that Anna had helped with finding useful information.

With that, lots of time that would have been spent hiding things from Theodore had been cut short. Now, all they needed to do was use that information to make meaningful moves.

The intense antiseptic smell greeted Amelia as she approached the patients' wards.

The nurses acknowledged her, and Amelia headed straight for the marked bed of Mr. Peter.

"Madam Amelia," the tiny voice of a female called out from behind. Amelia turned to see who it was.

"Oh, Jane," Amelia said. "Good to see you today."

"Good to see you too, madam. Are you here to check on anyone in particular?"

"Well, I would do an all-round check if I had the time, but I want to know how Mr. Peter from the textile factory is faring. Theodore wishes to have a personal report."

"Oh, we've restricted all visitors to Mr. Peter."

A frown formed across Amelia's face as she heard this.

"Why is this?"

"He is reacting poorly to the treatment he's receiving, and the symptoms seem to keep spreading, so we have limited access to those he needs the most. Specialist staff."

"This is not good. I have the right to see him, don't I?" Amelia asked, trying to see if she could use her position to visit Peter. "I mean, Master Theodore has specifically sent me. And of course, my dear husband would also like to know. We are worried about him."

"Well, nobody came to see him during all the time he has been here. With all due respect, it would have been better to arrive sooner. The poor soul has been all alone."

Amelia immediately took on a look of guilt. "I am so, so sorry. My husband, Andrew has had so much to do."

"Well, Theodore always managed to visit. No one has ever claimed to be busier than Theodore. The patients miss him. He knew them all by name, and their cases too."

"I'm sorry," Amelia said again. Now, she felt angry at Andrew for putting her in this position.

"I shall see what I can do," said Jane. "But if you enter, Master Theodore or Master Andrew needs to give this authorization first. He is in isolation. Not just anyone may wander in."

Amelia bit her lower lip as she thought of what to do.

"When is your shift over?"

"In the next three hours."

"Great. I will shortly return with my husband," Amelia said.

Her breathing pace had increased as she was concerned for Mr. Peter and wondered why she had not bothered about him herself before then. And if he died, Theodore would be livid.

"All right, madam," the nurse said. "I will be here to attend to you."

Amelia walked away as quickly as she could, her flat sandals creating echoing click-clack sounds as they hit the tiles in the hallway.

Once outside in the courtyard again, she ran as if her own life depended on it.

"Amelia!" Andrew said when she arrived at his place of work. "Right on time."

Amelia sat down, trying to catch her breath.

"If you had come a moment later, you may have missed us."

"Huh?"

"Anna set up a meeting with a potential client who just so happens to be here in Teleos for tourism purposes," Andrew said. "Is this young lady not a beautiful, wondrous blessing?"

"What?" Amelia was still trying to catch her breath so was unable to say much.

"A lead in one of the engineering firms is in Teleos as we speak. Catch your breath and prepare, please. This is it, darling."

"It has... it has to be tonight?"

"She is leaving first thing in the morning. That's what Anna says," Andrew said. He was already packing up his things. "So, we may not have an opportunity like this ever again."

"Andrew, wait," Amelia finally said. "The clinic says I need permission from you or Father to see Mr. Peter. You have to come with me. Right now."

"That can't be," Andrew said. This news did not seem to shock or surprise him. "You go there almost every day in the week and every doctor or nurse knows who you are. Plus, you are my wife. How dare they refuse to let you in, and therefore burden me this way! Go there and say—"

"I have just been there and I am telling you, you need to come with me!"

"Amelia, *you* need to come with *me*. This meeting will not last long.This woman is busy, and she came for a short rest period here in Teleos and we are about to give up the chance to arrange things with her. Surely, it won't take long."

Amelia stared back in confusion, trying to think of what to do, but there seemed to be no way out of the entire situation.

"And you will come back with me, so we see Mr. Peter? Together?"

"I have no other plans after the meeting, so I will be available for that."

By this time, he was already waiting for Amelia.

"All right," Amelia said. "You win." Under her breath, she huffed, "as you always do."

She stood, grabbed her bag from the couch, adjusted her clothing, and heaved a deep sigh.

"Here's to progress in Teleos," Andrew said, clutching Amelia's hand.

He led her outside.

"Oh, there you are," Andrew said with a large smile, seeing Anna waiting by a great tree.

Amelia looked to see Anna looking very nice indeed.

"You sure look like you are ready to change the world tonight."

"When duty calls, we answer," Anna said with a weak and unwilling smile. "Hello, Amelia."

"Hi, Anna." Amelia stepped outside and Phillip closed the door.

Andrew had arranged for Anna to take the rest of the day off simply because of this meeting that could not be rescheduled.

There was hardly ever a reason for Amelia to leave the vast structure that housed her home and her work. She had no family outside, so taking in the air was a highlight for her.

They walked many streets until Amelia was quite exhausted, finally coming to a low building among a gathering of fruit trees. They were escorted in, then settled into a large meeting area where aides wafted great fans made of enormous leaves.

But there were no refreshments, and a meeting would always have refreshments.

A table would usually already be sitting bedecked with goblets of wine and bread.

"So, you said she knows all about the project already?" Andrew asked as they settled in.

"Yes, I have briefed her on the basics, and she only agreed to meet because she thinks this is a splendid idea. She was surprised that someone in your position could see the future."

"Ah! When opportunity comes, best be prepared!" Andrew said, looking pleased with himself, seeing that things were connecting even better than he expected them to from the start.

He also liked it being said that he could see into the future. That was the kind of reputation he would be pleased to grow for himself. Andrew the great visionary... Andrew the seer.

"But why meet here when we could have met at the hostel where she is staying?" Amelia asked. "I mean, there are lots of spaces for meetings in the hostel. Why the need to leave the confines? Of the center of the city? I am exhausted before we even begin, and we need to get this over as soon as possible to go see Mr. Peter. He depends on us."

"Oh, hush. Relax, Amelia," Anna said. "We are not meeting right here. Oh no; we are awaiting a carriage to take us to the building. We are here in Teleos, your city.

"The lady is not right here, you see. The lady in question simply said she would only be free at this time, hence this, and hence we must meet her where she is. Her time is limited, so the least we can do is go where she suggests. It is the least we can do for her."

"Yes, all right," Amelia responded with a weary smile. The carriage came, and they climbed aboard. It was another bumpy ride out of the city.

Finally, Anna started to rise from her seat, and she cried out, "Here we are!"

She flung the door wide. But the sight that met their eyes should have terrified Andrew, because it terrified Amelia. She stood still for the next few seconds in complete shock, seeing Anna lead the way into the building as if magnetically drawn to it.

The glow from inside almost blinded Amelia. But Andrew seemed unfazed.

Chapter 9: Deception

"Andrew!" Amelia grabbed Andrew's arm and pulled him back. "Andrew, what are you doing?"

"What do you mean, what am I doing? We are here for the meeting, are we not?"

"Andrew, have you suddenly gone blind?" Amelia shrieked. "Look!"

Amelia pointed at the building in front of them, terrified.

Andrew looked in the direction in which she was pointing.

"What is wrong, Amelia?"

"Andrew, look around you. It's the same building Father has always warned us about." Amelia kept her hold on Andrew's hand.

"Amelia, do not be so dramatic. This is a chance for me to prove myself to Father."

"No, I'm not having it, Andrew. We should leave right now," Amelia said. Phillip had just stabled the carriage and horses and came around the corner.

"Amelia, this right here," Andrew said, pointing to the same building. "This is the key to riches and abundant prosperity here in Teleos. Through me, through us!

"As I have said, this will be the making of me in my father's eyes. This will become one of the greatest achievements in Teleos and beyond. This alone will cement the wonderful things I have done already for the city. It will put the cherry on the already iced cake!"

"When he finally determines what I have done, and all that I have achieved for my great city, he will be so happy he will jump for joy. Then I know he will let me make *all* the decisions."

"And that is enough reason to disobey Father?" she cried.

"How can you believe I disobey him? He tells me I am the ruler. So, let me rule."

"Is anything wrong?" Anna said, walking back to meet Amelia and Andrew. "We are almost behind schedule."

Amelia shot Anna a firm, hard look.

"Anna, what is in there?" Amelia asked. Her hands folded over her chest, waiting.

"It's just an eating house," Anna said. "Tables, stools."

"How do you know that?"

"Because I have been here before. Come on, I don't want to spoil this. What's the matter?"

"No, there's nothing," Andrew said. "Just give us a minute."

"But I don't know how long she will wait," Anna replied, stepping forward to give Amelia and Andrew enough space for a private conversation.

"Andrew, Father would not like this," Amelia said. "Deep down you know this. Something terrible awaits us in there. Something that will destroy everything!"

"I think Father knew a day like this would come and he would rather just remain in control," Andrew said firmly. "So, he put rules in place. Rules that would still give him control."

"Andrew, but what if you are wrong? What if this all falls apart?"

"Why the pessimism? What if I am right? I have not seen or experienced anything wrong since we started building this idea. Please, have some trust in your husband."

"I just... I just need this to go well so we can get it over with."

"Then we should just get on with it. We are here now, and we need tangible information to be able to successfully sell this to Father. Wait and see."

Amelia closed her eyes, taking in a few deep breaths. She had no choice in the matter.

Her husband may not yet rule Teleos fully. But in their household, he ruled.

"Let's do this," she said.

Anna was still waiting for them at the door and when she saw them walking toward her, with Andrew carrying his autonomous bot plans on thick parchment.

She opened the door wide enough so they could go in.

"You can wait outside, Phillip," Andrew said. "It will not take long."

"As you like, Mr. Andrew," Phillip said. "I'll be here if you need anything."

The three walked in gracefully, leaving Phillip alone outside. He found a place to sit.

"Looks like we got here earlier than scheduled?" Amelia said, looking around and feeling uneasy at how the entire place was set up. It was extremely dark on the inside, a great contrast to the bright light Amelia had always seen from the view of the mansion.

The chairs were oddly shaped, and similar bizarre antiques were spread over the house.

"No," a feminine voice said, filling their ears. "You are just in time."

"Who was that?" Andrew asked. "Where did that come from?"

"That is our host," Anna said. "She is here for the meeting."

"Our host? But... but where is the lady we agreed to meet?"

"Thank you, Morana," the same voice said. A figure appeared in front of a second door in the room, a door that seemed to lead to the inner room or the kitchen of this 'eating house.'

"Morana?" Amelia said. "Who is Morana?"

A woman now walked in their direction, over-dressed for the meeting.

Her silky black hair was packed into a tight bun and placed nicely at the back of her head, and the deep red robe she wore stood out in the dark, adding to her refined beauty. Black jewels adorned her neck and her hands and arms, all the way to the elbows.

"Good evening and thank you for seeing us at such short notice," Andrew said.

He stood, outstretching his hand.

"The pleasure is all mine," she said, taking his hand and holding it for longer than one would normally do. "You must be Andrew, son of Master Theodore?"

"Yes. Yes, I am," Andrew said. "And you are?"

"Call me Selena," the lady said, letting go of Andrew's hand and turning her gaze to Amelia. "And you must be the wife."

"I... I am," Amelia said. "My name is Amelia."

"Very nice to meet you both," Selena said, walking slowly, as though she glided.

The only thing that gave off her steps was the sound of her fine leather sandals slapping against the tiled ground. "Thank you for bringing them to me, Morana."

Anna sat in a corner and nodded her head.

Amelia replayed the name in her head, overtaken by shock and some sense of fear.

She had never guessed that Anna's full name was Morana. Surely, she should have known this with the amount of time spent together when they were younger.

"My cousin runs this place. Forgive the ambiance. She likes serenity and quiet," Selena said. "So, I asked that we have it for the night if that is fine by you. We do not want anyone listening in on all the important things we will discuss today, eh?"

"Sure," Andrew said, becoming more excited. "You are right about that."

Amelia looked unsure. *All the important things* sounded like quite a long list of topics that might take a very long time to discuss. And they did not have long at all. She was still thinking of and worrying about poor Mr. Peter, and the nurse waiting for them to go visit.

"Great." Selena walked over to a ledge from which she fetched two fine red goblets and a thick water jug. She returned to the table where they sat.

"So, Anna says you can help us with bringing in autonomous bots to Teleos," Andrew said suddenly. He wondered why so much time was already being wasted on saying nothing.

"Here, you need to drink something," Selena said, pouring the first of the goblets. "I need you both relaxed because it is crucial we make only the right decisions here today."

Amelia wished to turn this down, but she really *was* thirsty and needed to calm down.

After the race to find Andrew, she had not gotten the chance to take any water to calm herself.

But how could she be sure this was water? What if this was some poisoned chalice?

She reassured herself, telling herself not to be so dramatic again.

"Thank you very much," Amelia said, and Selena then poured her a goblet full and watched her gulp down its contents.

"Would you like some?"

"No, not yet," Andrew said eagerly, wanting to get down to business.

"As you wish," Selena said. She replaced the stopper in the water jug and took a seat. "How about we have some background talk about Teleos?"

"Huh?" Andrew said, looking at Amelia, who had become a little quiet.

"These partners of mine will require me to know a bit about a city we plan on collaborating with. I am sure you understand this?" Selena said.

"Yes, of course," Andrew replied. "What would you like to know?"

"All that I can know," Selena said. "The more information I take back, the more chance I have of persuading my partners. Isn't that how it works?"

Andrew's eyes locked with hers and he just kept staring, saying nothing. There was something about her, something unusual.

Something he had never seen in the people of Teleos. But maybe it was only that the people here were more forward-thinking. After all, they were willing to develop autonomous bots!

Yes, that must be it.

"I think that glass of water would help you relax a bit, honey," Amelia whispered. "I feel great after mine! In fact, I might take another. It must be blessed water, from a holy well."

Andrew looked at Amelia, and she looked better, more relaxed, with a calm look.

"May I?" Selena looked at Andrew for confirmation as she held the thick jug of water.

"Sure," Andrew said, as he picked up the goblet right after she filled it, emptying its contents into his mouth and not sparing as much as a single drop.

"So, back to our discussion," Selena said. "You were going to tell me about your city."

"Right," Andrew said. He swallowed hard as he felt a little dizzy, but shook his head to get over it, concluding it must have been because of how dark the room was. "There is not much to say. I just think my father does not have what it takes anymore to rule this city."

Amelia looked taken back at that, but oddly, she found herself nodding along.

"Hmm," Selena said. "And you wish to?"

"Of course. I would love to. Who wouldn't? Besides, it is my birthright, just as Theodore has been telling me all along. I never wished to rule at first. He insisted. Starting with these autonomous bots, I now intend to, and I'm sure the change will blow him off his feet. That is why we have come."

"Well, you would certainly surprise him. Do you not even realize Theodore has dreaded this day from the very beginning? Has that thought not struck you yet?"

"Theodore?" Andrew said. His vision had failed and needed the table for support. His head felt woolly, as if stuffed with tiny cotton balls and dandelion seeds.

"Theodore stopped you from coming into this very building. Am I right?" she asked. "No doubt he warned you of the building with the brightest lights in the city."

Andrew looked around himself as if he had only just noticed his environment.

"Yes. Yes, he did. He said to stay away from the building and to never venture inside," Andrew said. "And it wasn't just one time. He said it so many times, I was thinking he was becoming quite mad. As if his sanity had abandoned him. There's nothing wrong with this place."

"So, he did not tell you *why* you should never come near the building?"

"He said it would bring destruction to me and to the whole of Teleos. It would destroy everything we had built." Andrew laughed and burped. "Destruction indeed," he added.

"Well, I do not see the city falling, and neither are you," Selena said. She looked at Anna and Amelia, whose eyes were fixed on her. "Theodore never wanted you to rise above him. That's what he meant by destruction. You have surely seen how controlling your father is. I'll wager he promised you the chance to rule, then has prevented you from doing so at every turn."

"I knew it! What did I tell you, Amelia?" Andrew said, holding his wife's hands. "This is the beginning of our much-delayed reign. See, our hostess speaks the greatest truths!"

"And you will lead even better than he ever did, starting with the autonomous bots that you have so wonderfully brought up," Selena added quickly. "People say he is a progressive man…"

"He is nowhere near as progressive as I intend to be!" said Andrew, up on his feet and punching the air. He was almost shouting. Amelia, too, stood tall and shouted, "Yes!"

"And you would help me—us—make that a reality?" Andrew said.

"Step by step, all the way."

Andrew smiled and poured himself another glass of water, gulping it down in one hit, and turned back to Selena.

"What do I need to do?" he asked.

"Tell me everything about Teleos. I need to know the deep details that Theodore shares with you and only you."

Andrew stayed quiet and looked Selena in the eye. He was weighing her up again, at the same time as attempting to stop his head from spinning.

Why would she wish to know all this? It was not what they had come for.

"Is that necessary?" he asked. "Andrew, I am doing this to help you; to make you the true leader of Teleos. The more you divulge to me, the better you can gain control of it all." "I mean, we should get down to the autonomous bot business, should we not? That was the whole point of this meeting, wasn't it?"

"We will get to that soon. This is important to achieve right now. I'm trying to help you become greater than your father, but in order for me to do that, I must know what makes him great. Then we can aim to disrupt his rule with ours. I mean, yours. You see, I need to program all this into your autonomous bots."

"Hmm," Andrew said. "I understand now."

The time that followed was filled with Andrew's hoarse voice. He spoke calmly at first but proceeded to shout and scream about all that upset him and how much of a better ruler than his father he would be if only the man would stick to his word and let him rule.

Amelia felt so mellow by now, partaking of the fine spring water or well water, whatever it was. She thought of it as magic water. Each time her goblet sat empty, Selena filled it.

Amelia had not felt so relaxed in a long time and was relishing every moment here.

It must be correct what her husband said, that Theodore disliked anyone coming here because they were no longer under his control when they departed Teleos city, out of his line of sight and the view of his spies and watchful technology screens.

Their ruler was a total control freak! They saw it all now.

Amelia spoke occasionally, backing all that Andrew said with proof of how hard they had both worked to bring Teleos to where it was today.

She also told Selena and Anna the concern they had for the elderly and sick.

"Tell me about the gold," Selena said.

She looked very calm and relaxed, but above all, she seemed deeply satisfied.

"The gold! Well, it all comes from Havilah," Andrew said. "It flows like a river. You would get lots of it and go unnoticed if you..." He coughed loudly and reached for the goblet again.

"If you what?" Selena pushed. "Speak up!"

"If you can get to the control room in his quarters," Andrew said. "Everything he needs to rule the city is in there."

"Hmm."

"Why do you need to know this?"

"Oh, you do. Not me, but you, Andrew, will have complete access *and* ownership of the control room in no time. I told you—I need to program all this into the autonomous bots. The autonomous bots can only assist if they know everything, you see? They are only as capable as the information we put into them."

"But I always need my father's help to know things. He alone knows the way around it all."

"And that is why he stopped you from coming in here," Selena said. "So, it stays that way, and he never gets to leave the position of the ruler."

"Ah! I see," Andrew said. "But it is all over now."

"All thanks to you," Andrew said.

"Because of what you have told me so far, I can now program all this into the autonomous bots and they can begin to find out the rest for themselves."

He leaned back and put his hands behind his head, looking at the ceiling.

"Excuse me for a moment," Selena said. She stood and started to walk back through the other doorway from which she had come. "Please come with me, Morana."

Anna stood and followed her.

"Darling, is this great news?" Andrew said, clapping his hands together in excitement. "We will take Teleos to even greater heights. Father will be so proud."

"That would be great," Amelia replied.

Andrew was nodding, enthused and excited by it all. "Selena will help us get to the top and when we are there, it will be impossible to overthrow us."

"Are you sure about this?" Amelia asked. She felt very drowsy, and she put her head on the table to rest. "You think that would work? I must sleep, dearest husband. Must... sleep."

"Yes, a hundred percent positive. When have I ever let you down, darling? I am so tired too. It must be the exhaustion of such great news coming my way."

He also slumped forward, resting his head on the table.

Chapter 10: A Strange Place

By the time Amelia and Andrew regained consciousness and became aware of their surroundings, time was far spent. Amelia was the first to wake from her sleep, stretching her arms above her head and looking around to see that she was in a very unfamiliar place.

"Andrew," Amelia whispered, tugging at Andrew's shirt as he lay fast asleep beside her. "Andrew, wake up."

"Hmm." Andrew took some time before realizing they were somewhere strange. "What the...? Where are we? What is this place?"

"I thought *you* would know," Amelia said, more or less back to her usual self. Her heart was thumping and not just because she felt afraid here. "Andrew, we need to leave now. I... I promised the nurse we would return to see dear Mr. Peter. So that we could please, Father."

"To hell with Father!" cried Andrew, then he seemed to come to his senses. "Ah. Yes. No, you are right, we must please, Father." He seemed quite shocked by his outburst, as if unplanned.

"Where is Phillip?" Andrew asked, wiping his eyes with the back of his hands and looking around himself again, hoping to remember how he had got there in the first place.

"How about we find out when we leave? I don't feel comfortable here, Andrew. Do you? How did we get here, anyway?"

Standing, Amelia felt an itch on her arm suddenly.

"Here," she said. "Hold my hand."

She stretched her right hand forward to help Andrew up from the chair. After much strain and effort, they were both on their feet, although a little unsteady, looking around the dark room.

"Come. That door should lead us outside," Andrew said, staggering toward the door and as he pushed it open, it gave way. The light outside of the building was blinding.

Both had to raise their hands to shield their eyes, affecting their stance even more.

Before they made it outside fully, Andrew noticed inscriptions on the wall. He stared hard to make sense of it and when he finally did, his heart raced faster than ever.

"Amelia, we need to hurry."

"Where is Phillip?" Amelia asked. "He should be here, right? This is getting worse."

The bright light kept piercing their eyes, preventing them from seeing their way and restricting what they could see ahead.

"Phillip! Phillip, where are you?" Andrew shouted, still shielding his eyes.

"Sir!" Phillip called out from the corner "Yes, sir," Phillip said. "Just stay here and I'll bring the carriage and horses around." "Yes, but please hurry. We need to get out of this building. "I'm here. To your right."

"Get the carriage now, and get us out of here," Andrew shouted, even though he felt weak and was shaken from his ordeal.

here, Phillip."

As they got into the carriage, Andrew looked back at the building and his face fell in shame. He buried his face in his hands and ran his hand through his hair.

"What have I done? What the hell have I done? I have failed father," Andrew said. "I have failed myself. I have failed the people of Teleos. I have failed you. I have failed us all!"

Amelia stayed quiet for the entirety of the journey home, replaying all that had happened over again in her head, thinking hard, trying to remember where she had gone wrong, what she had done to get so carried away.

"Phillip," she said. "How long were we in there?"

Phillip looked in the rearview mirror to see Amelia's face. It was a bit swollen, and she looked like she had gone through a great deal.

"The best part of the day, ma'am," Phillip replied quietly.

"Oh, my goodness!" Amelia cried out. "That long!"

She wished she could console her husband, but even she felt a heavy deal of guilt.

When they arrived at the building, they saw it was isolated, as all the factory workers had finished for the day. "Go to the rear of the building," Andrew said.

"Sir?"

"Take the back way into the building, Phillip," Andrew said. "The back stairs."

Amelia sobbed quietly in her seat. She curled up and looked out of the window, wishing she could turn back the hands of time. Wiping her eyes with the back of her hands, she sobbed.

"Amelia," Andrew started. "We need to stay strong. We are rulers."

"I doubt that," she said. "Rulers of what? We have brought about the downfall of Teleos! *You* have brought the downfall, I should say. *You* got us into this mess."

Andrew went quiet and began to think as Phillip trotted the carriage around the building and, after a short time, they came to a stop in front of the rear stairs.

"Phillip," Andrew said, picking up his parchments and holding them close.

"Yes, Mr. Andrew."

"There is no reason for my father to know the matters of today, is there?"

Phillip went quiet and avoided eye contact with Andrew as he knew he was looking at him through the rearview mirror.

"Phillip, I asked a question!" Andrew said at the top of his voice. "Is there any need for my father to know the matters of the night?"

"No sir, there is none," Phillip said.

Amelia could see Andrew holding his hands together in fear.

"That would be all for the night," Andrew said. "And don't forget, not a word to my father about tonight. Let's go, Amelia."

Amelia said nothing. She had nothing to say and even if she did; she felt weak in her stomach. She opened the door, planting her feet on the graveled ground.

"Do you need some help?" Phillip asked, seeing the issue with their unsteadiness.

"No, we will manage, Phillip," Andrew replied. "Come, Amelia, hold on to my arm."

"This can't be that bad," Andrew said quietly as they finally made it up the stairs. "There is no real damage. There can't be." He spoke to himself, trying to shake off the fear.

He felt like an unwelcome stranger in his own home, holding Amelia's hands as they crept up the stairs like a thief with his ally in tow.

Amelia wished she could respond, but all she could do was think of the events, replay them in her mind, and try to make sense of them. First, she had tried convincing Andrew that they should not go into the building, but then she was inside, agreeing to everything he was blurting out.

Had she really been supporting him to whatever he was doing??

Had she really been nodding along and shouting "yes!" to his preposterous suggestions?

And then they had woken, not knowing how long they had slept for.

As soon as they entered through their own doorway, they both dropped on the chaise longue.

"Father does not have to know, Amelia," Andrew said. They had both been quiet for a long time, staying still and saying nothing to each other. "He does not, I assure you."

"Have you assured yourself, Andrew?" Amelia said. "Are you sure that you have convinced yourself of this? Because I have to let you know you have convinced me of nothing."

For the first time since their marriage, she was being an argumentative wife.

"Y-yes, of course," Andrew said. "I-I mean, just some days ago, he was barely available for us, you know? Don't you remember?"

Andrew burped, and a pungent smell escaped from his mouth.

"What did you drink there?" Amelia asked. "Or, what did *we* drink?"

"I wish I knew. First, we got there, and all I felt was high energy to get all the information we needed for the autonomous bots," Andrew said. "Next, she served us some liquid to ease our stress."

"Yes," Amelia agreed.

Her eyes opened as Andrew spoke because she could not quite remember the entire detail of the night, but things were slowly coming back to her.

"Yes, that's right. I remember having the drink. Selena was determined for us to drink."

"Yes! Yes, then I start talking and talking about everything," Andrew said. "Oh no, I said so much. I know I did. Why did I go there?"

Amelia turned sharply to Andrew.

"Andrew, there is one very important question neither of us has yet asked."

"Which is?"

"Anna. Where is she?" Amelia asked. "She asked all the questions, right? Anna set up the meeting. It was Anna who came to our home that morning. I knew there was something amiss."

"Yes, Anna set up everything. You're right.Why did she do that, though?" Andrew said.

"The lady. The meeting. It was all made up. We did not meet with any lady."

Andrew could hear the anger in her voice.

" Did you see anyone else but Anna in the room back there?" she went on.

"No. There was no one else," Andrew said. "It was just us three."

Amelia lay back on the couch and looked at the ceiling. "I knew something was different about Anna. I could tell, but you would not listen to me. You were too engrossed in your autonomous bots and your sense of narcissism and self-importance."

"Amelia, this is no time to throw the blame at each other, all right?" Andrew shot back. "And besides, I was extremely conscious of every-thing I said in there until *you* convinced me to drink whatever it was in that cup, you know? *You* drank from it before I did."

Amelia said nothing. She heaved a deep sigh and sat up again.

"Maybe there is no real damage done," Andrew said gently.

"What?"

"It does not look or feel like anything has gone wrong, has it?" Andrew asked. "We both escaped intact. Father shall know of none of it. So, why are we so fretful?"

"What do you mean? We just disobeyed the one and only thing Father repeatedly warned us to never do," Amelia said. "Think about it. Think of how many times he told us to never go near."

"Yes, that is right. But if Phillip keeps this away from Father, all is well."

"Oh, come on, Andrew. Father will find out. Don't forget, he still keeps his hand in with the running of Teleos, and its people respect him more than ever."

"If you stay quiet, I stay quiet, and Phillip stays quiet, I do not see how he would find out."

Amelia thought about this. She bit her lower lip, thinking of what Andrew had just said.

"What about Anna?" Amelia asked. "What if she tells Father herself?"

"She would be damned to do such," Andrew replied. "She would never do that. She fooled us, deceived us into going to the forbidden building. I do not see how telling Father would favor her. That blasted woman! I knew I should never have trusted her!"

"You mean the wondrous, beautiful woman who had you saying you were blessed?"

"Yes, that one," he admitted, looking sheepish. But how dare his wife argue with him?

Amelia's thoughts were filled with a lot of things.

"Andrew, do you remember what Father said way back about finding our way back to him at the slightest inconvenience?"

"Yes, I remember many things Father said to us."

"Andrew!" she shouted. "We must tell Father about this."

"What?"

"Yes! Father says to us all the time that when we feel lost, we should find our way back to him! He promised that he would not leave us to ourselves as long as we report everything. So, we need to tell him everything, and quickly."

"Are you out of your mind?" Andrew said to Amelia. "We are not just feeling lost, Amelia. We are already lost! We have done what we should have neverdone, but this is different!"

Amelia went quiet. The shock was great, as he had never spoken to her in such a manner.

More than ever, she wished she had spoken up about Andrew's obsession with the autonomous bots even after the meeting with Theodore.

"Please forgive me for how I spoke, Amelia," Andrew said. "I am deeply confused about this, and my mind is not with my heart at this time. I speak, but it is not the real me."

"I understand," Amelia said. "Nor am I myself," she agreed. "Maybe if I had told Father about your obsession with autonomous bots. Maybe if I had taken it up that there was something different about Anna when I met her. Maybe if I had held you down and taken you by the hand to come with me to the clinic, maybe none of these terrible things would have happened.

"Maybe, just maybe!!"

"Please, Amelia, don't put so much load on your shoulder," Andrew said. "If you do that, what do I do with myself, seeing how much effort I put into this? How much I allowed power and greed to sit in my heart and turn me away from my father's instructions?"

The air felt still, as though all the windows in the room were shut. Sharon must have retired for the day, seeing that they did not come back home hours after they normally would.

After minutes of silence, Andrew stood and walked to the window as if he had read Amelia's mind. Opening it, the air rushed into the room, spreading a feeling of greater calm around.

Andrew walked back to Amelia and helped her up.

"Come on," he said. "Let us go to wash and eat. Tomorrow is another busy day."

"Very busy indeed," Amelia said. "First thing, we must head to the clinic to see how Mr. Peter is faring and carry on all the activities we have missed out on."

"Yes, yes. Mr. Peter," Andrew said. He heaved a deep sigh and led Amelia to the bedroom.

"I'll take a hot fragranced bath first, if you don't mind?" Amelia said.

"Of course. We can have dinner once I've bathed, too."

The moon was high as they settled to eat, surprising both, as they did not realize that so much time had passed. "I think we should shut the windows," Amelia said as they ate.

She had been picking on her food since they started and had barely gone halfway.

"Are you cold?"

"Shivering, actually." She wrapped her robe tighter around her body and tucked herself into the space under the dining table.

Standing, Andrew patted her shoulder, then walked to close the window.

As he spread the curtains apart, a look of confusion came across his features.

"What is taking so long, Andrew?" Amelia said, still picking on her meal.

Andrew stayed quiet, peering out through the window, not saying a word.

"Is anything the matter?" Amelia asked. When she turned around and saw that he wasn't making any movement to respond to her questions, she walked toward him.

"Why are you so quiet?" Amelia asked again.

She moved the curtain away and tugged on Andrew's arm.

"Look," Andrew finally said. He had closed the window halfway, so the cold air whistled as it found its way into the room. Andrew pointed ahead so Amelia could see what he had seen.

"What is it?"

"There, down there," he replied. "Look, just there."

He pointed in the general direction.

Amelia followed the direction of his hand and after a few seconds of searching, she finally saw what he was talking about. The lights in Teleos were bright and lighted the streets as usual, but something was off. The lights that shone ever so brightly at the extreme of the city had now dimmed. Every other day, it had looked ever so beautiful, attractive, and it had taken a lot of consciousness to stay away from it, but now, it was difficult to see that a building stood there.

"How... How did that happen?" Amelia asked. She stared on, squinting to see if there was anything there at all, but the darkness of the night was thick.

"I wish I could give an answer," Andrew said. His mood had fallen again.

He had tried to shake off the guilt he felt, saying loudly to himself that his father would never find out, but now, he was not so sure.

The couple just stood there, oblivious to the amount of time passing. When Andrew had seen enough, when it had truly sunk in, he walked away from the window and Amelia followed silently behind, retiring for the day to their bedrooms in a bid to find sleep.

To Andrew's surprise, Amelia's eyes shone ever so brightly even with the amount of stress they were both under; her mind was full, and he could tell she must be trying to figure out what they had done, but so was he. After all, it had been Andrew's idea to attend the meeting.

He wished he could comfort her and make her feel better, less guilty, but even he needed that.

Instead, he thought of ways to get out of the mess they had gotten into.

He had no idea of the amount of damage he had caused, and what exactly had been affected by his stupidity. He still felt a little dizzy from whatever it was they had drunk, but he was sure there would be more repercussions.

Father would definitely find out if he already hadn't. The night passed slowly, and Andrew's mind worked overtime, but for all the wrong reasons. On the occasion in the past when he couldn't sleep,he would usually start thinking positive thoughts about the day ahead.

But this was different.

He had disobeyed his father's direct order, and he would face the punishment of it for sure.

Chapter 11: The Curse

Theodore sat on his large chair in the dining hall in his chambers, staring into space. Once again, he had taken a step back from the general running of the factory and the welfare of those in the city, attempting to get some much needed rest. After the last meeting with Andrew and Amelia, he felt confident that Andrew would do nothing to displease him, and from the reports he had gotten from Michael so far, things seemed to be running extremely well, even in his absence.

It was almost spring, a time in the year when leaders in neighboring cities surrounding Teleos would gather to celebrate how the city had progressed.

Aside from the unity and love in the city of Teleos, the festival of the spring was something that bonded the entire city and those farther afield, celebrating the various cultures and foods native to each city. It made Theodore happy, and of course, made all his people happy too.

Due to it being the largest and most resourceful of all the cities involved in this alliance, Teleos had always been the grand sponsor and host of this show.

"Michael," Theodore called out. "Are you there?"

"No, Master. He left early this morning to receive reports," Uriel answered.

"I thought he had received them already?"

"No, he has about three more rounds after this," Uriel said, stepping out into the light and standing in front of Theodore.

"Very well," Theodore said. "I need more letters sent out again today, reminding each city leader of the annual meeting we are holding in two days' time to prepare for spring."

"That would make it three reminders we have sent, Master," Uriel said.

"Make it four, if needed," Theodore said. "Every single thing has to be perfect. It *needs* to be perfect, Uriel."

"Yes, of course, Master. I was just informing you we usually only send the original invite and a single reminder, not three."

"Do you think I don't know that, Uriel?" Theodore said. "This year's festival will be the first where Andrew will be introduced to the many leaders from the neighboring cities and also, if you need reminding, it will be the first time the festival has taken place since the completion of the gold mansion. So, as you now understand, I want everything to be perfect."

"Yes, Master," Uriel said. He started to leave when Theodore summoned him again.

"Would you stop by my son's workroom at the factory, please? Tell him I need to see him and his wife tonight when the stars emerge. It's very important. Tell him not to be late."

"As you like, Master," Uriel said.

"You may go," Theodore said. He stood from his chair and walked to the large double window in the corner of the dining room. Staring through, he heaved a deep sigh.

The beneficial work he had started in Teleos stood firm, the structure unshaken. He thought about how hard Andrew had worked, and it brought joy to his heart. Joy and lots of pride.

My son, with whom I am very well pleased. He has done well, to my surprise, admittedly.

And his wife too, she keeps him on the straight and even path.

The sky was bright and birds of various sizes and colors flew, adding even more color to the already beautiful Teleos. Theodore could have stayed there indefinitely, admiring and soaking it all in. The sun had risen, and the streets below were already getting busy.

Then he heard his favorite sound of the day, the machines in the factory powering up .

As Theodore continued to take all of this in and admire his beloved city, the door to his quarters flung open and Michael strode in briskly.

"Good morning, Master," Michael said. With how loudly his voice echoed, one would think he was taking lessons from Theodore himself.

"It has been two days," Theodore said.

"Yes, Master. I traveled out of Teleos to Havilah and Cush to fetch the final reports."

"Good. Drop them in my study and come back immediately."

Michael hurried away, holding the tablet, and soon returned to Theodore's quarters.

"Now, Michael," Theodore said. "I need you to go around the factory, starting from my son's room, announcing that we will have visitors in the city in two days, and for that reason, the factory will not be operating for the next week."

"Yes, Master," Michael said.

Rather than leave immediately, he stood in front of Theodore.

"Is there a reason you are still here?" Theodore asked. "Do I need to explain to you again?"

"No, Master. There's an urgent report you need to attend to."

"And what does it entail?" Theodore was losing patience. "Just a quick summary."

"The gold harvests in Havilah are running down."

"What do you mean, running down?" Theodore asked, concerned but not worried.

"The city leaders have asked for some time to come up with an explanation for what is happening, but for now, he is just as confused as we are."

"How much has gone?"

"Almost two tons of gold in one night," Michael said shakily.

"We will deal with this after the gathering of the city leaders and before the festival of the spring," Theodore said firmly. His voice was unshaken, not because he cared little for the city, but because he knew Teleos would always bounce back.

"O-okay, Master," Michael said. He left the room hurriedly, without looking back.

He did not want to seem weak before his Master Theodore, but he was afraid for the well-being of Teleos at large. There were other pressing issues aside from the disappearance of the city's gold from a tightly secure area in Havilah. But he had not mentioned them.

He was afraid to speak out, fearing that this time, all hope was lost for Teleos.

Andrew and Amelia arrived at work that morning. It was the fifth time in a row that they would arrive extremely early, simply because they needed as many things sorted as possible.

Phillip was always around to assist them, and rather than simply hearing reports being read, Andrew took to following up on them all by himself. Before Phillip even brought up issues, Andrew often knew about them and would start making moves to get them cleared out.

"I think that would be the end of that matter, yes?" Andrew said to Phillip.

There had been a shortage in the quantity of dyes delivered from Starlight, and the company claimed they were not to blame. They were only working off the number ordered.

"Well, yes," Phillip replied. "They have been paid in full, but we still do not know where the shortage came from. We have barely any dyes, but we have spent more than usual. "

"Hmm. This doesn't make sense."

"The package was sealed by the time we got there, and the only reason Starlight was still paid in full was for the sake of the relationship we have built with them. We didn't want to jeopardize all the hard work we have put in, and they are usually a trustworthy supplier."

"I think we can sort this out later when we cleared other things up, hmm?" Andrew walked over to the dispenser in the corner of the room and helped himself to a cup.

"Yes, Master," Phillip said.

"Is there anything else?"

"More people are falling sick with an illness. The doctors could not explain what it is. They are doing all they can, but can't seem to find a breakthrough."

"Phillip," Andrew started. "You have said many times to allow the doctors to do what they are paid for. We have more important things to worry about right now."

"Yes, sire."

"A solution will be found, and it will be over. It must be food poisoning, I suppose. Or some sort of virus—"

"Are you free?" Amelia interrupted. "Do you think you can put aside some time for me?"

"Of course. You know I always will. What is it?"

"Can we visit the clinic together, please?" Amelia said. "It has been a while, and the nurse says the same thing each time I go there that Mr. Peter has been placed under close monitoring."

"I don't believe this. You *still* have not been able to see Mr. Peter?" Andrew asked, a little irritated. "I thought this was sorted days ago."

"I thought so too, but they denied me access again. I still need either your or Father's permission. As I said, they were expecting me to come with you on the day we—"

"Yes, yes. Stop harping on about the day we went to... where we should not have gone!"

As much as Andrew adored his wife, she was irritating him a lot these days. She was talking back to him too, something no ruler should ever tolerate.

Andrew looked over his table as if in search of something.

"We can be on our way now," Andrew said. "It shouldn't take too long."

"Great, thank you," Amelia replied, walking toward the door with Andrew following behind.

"Phillip, please keep an eye open for anything that happens while I am out," Andrew said.

He left and shut the door behind himself.

When they had walked a good distance away from the office, Amelia looked around to be sure no one was close enough to hear before she spoke.

"Andrew, I'm starting to worry now."

"Nonsense, everything will be fine, I promise."

"I'm not too sure about that. Uriel, Father's worker, was at the house this morning," she said.

"What? When?"

"You were in the bath, and I heard a knock on the door. Several knocks, in fact."

"You answered?"

"Of course not," Amelia said. "He stood there for a couple of minutes and finally left a note at the doorstep before leaving."

Andrew sighed. He knew what the note must have said. It had been well over a week since they had last held a meeting with Father. He had asked for some alone time again for about three days in a row, but afterward, they had come up with lots of excuses to stay away from him.

"I think Father will sense that there is an issue if we do not meet with him soon," Amelia said. "I mean, we used to meet with him every night and I do miss him."

"I think he will *know* that there is an issue if we *do not* meet with him soon," Andrew shot back. "Listen, we are taking time to clean up the traces of our absence from the matters of Teleos. If we do this well enough, there would not be any proof for him to know how we disobeyed."

Amelia thought about this. There was some sense in what he had said, even if she didn't agree. They continued to tiptoe to the clinic, finding their way to the nurses' ward.

"Good morning, Master," a plump, light-skinned lady said as she sighted Andrew and Amelia from afar. She wore a protective garment as she walked around. "To what do we owe the pleasure of your humble visit here today? We rarely see you in these parts. Not like Theodore."

Andrew looked around the clinic. It was not his favorite place to be, so when Amelia had first shown an unwavering interest in matters related to healthcare; he was truly pleased.

She could take over the handling of reports from there.

"Mr. Peter," Andrew said. "Allow us to see him, please."

The nurse looked at Andrew, then Amelia, and back at Andrew again.

"Master, we have not been able to find the cause of Mr. Peter's illness yet and we are trying to contain this, so it does not spread or affect the rest of Teleos."

"We would go in to meet him, not expect him to be brought to us."

"Yes, Master, I understand," the nurse replied. Her voice shook a little, and she hoped he would not get upset by her answers. "But we have admitted others with the same symptoms and we fear it is already spreading. We would rather no one sees him except those treating him."

Andrew did not want to push any further. He understood where the nurse was coming from, and he did not want to put her or the people of the city at any further risk.

"So be it. Have a good day ahead," Andrew said, grabbing Amelia's hand and turned around.

"Thank you, Master," the nurse said, scurrying away just in case Andrew changed his mind.

"Why did you do that? What did you gain by saying that?" Amelia asked. "What do we say to Father when he asks about Mr. Peter, which he inevitably will?"

"We tell him what the clinic says," Andrew said. "You should not bother yourself about little matters. Mr. Peter is in the best place."

"Sometimes, Andrew, I can't understand what goes on in your mind."

"I haven't let you down yet, Amelia, and I have no intention of doing so. Anyway, how would Father have felt if we had spread a terrible plague that would bring down the city?"

She looked awfully glum and stayed silent, biting her lip.

"Ha!" he laughed. "I would not be so dumb as to bring about the downfall of Teleos."

"I am sure," she said. Her face said the opposite.

They slowly walked back to work, pondering on different matters.

Andrew searched his mind to see if there was any stone left unturned, and they agreed to cut the pretense of being busy and finally see Theodore.

Andrew needed everything to go very well. Amelia, on the other hand, was concerned about Mr. Peter. She had spent weeks in the clinic and there had never been a case of isolation so intense that no one could visit but the doctors.

She hoped more than anything that he would recover soon. Very soon.

"Hello, Andrew," a familiar voice called out when Andrew and Amelia reached the door.

Standing a few meters away was Anna, looking almost the same as she had on the day she had led them to the building called Abaddon. The only difference was the apron she now wore.

"You! What are you doing here, you little witch?" Andrew said, charging toward her. Anna did not move back one step. She stayed still and watched as Amelia held Andrew back.

A few passersby stopped, wondering what on earth was going on.

"Hold on, Andrew," Amelia said. "Just give her a moment." She turned to Anna and looked her in the eye, trying to see if there was anything hypnotic about her.

"It is good to see you both again," Anna said, struggling to hold a large bag over her left shoulder. "I have been missing my dear friends. Have you not missed me?"

"Let us talk inside, shall we?" Amelia wore a fake, weak smile. "We mustn't create a scene."

Anna nodded and led the way, with Amelia and Andrew following.

They exchanged confused glances with one another, but did not say one word.

"Can you give us a moment, Phillip?" Andrew asked when he got into the office. Without being offered, Anna took a disposable cup and fetched herself some drinking water from the dispenser. Phillip nodded and walked from the room without uttering a word.

"So, you both did not think to search for me since that very day, eh?" Anna blurted as soon as the door closed. "You did not care about my welfare or whereabouts, you just wanted your hands clean, and without me in the way."

Andrew laughed bitterly, shaking his head and staring at Anna.

"How dare you! You come to this city, *our* city, causing much turmoil and disarray in such a short time, and you have the guts to ask for care and attention? Are you out of your mind?"

"Andrew." Amelia looked at him and shook her head, signaling for him to control himself.

"I have nothing against either of you," Anna said. "I do not know what happened back there at Abaddon. I simply came bearing good news."

Andrew laughed again, as though he had just heard a silly joke.

"*You* bring good news?" he said. "You? Morana? Oh, please enlighten me on this *good news*. I really cannot wait for this."

"My name is Anna," Anna shot back. "I have not come to exchange words with any of you. I only have something that you may take an interest in."

Without waiting for another word, Anna placed the bag down and revealed its contents.

"Here is what I have been working on since I disappeared," Anna said, pointing to the device on the table. It looked like a small machine, and Andrew and Amelia sat still and watched.

Holding a small remote control, Anna clicked a button and this small machine started whirring, within seconds transforming into a miniature autonomous bot.

Andrew moved back in shock when he saw what had happened.

"This... This is impressive,' Andrew said, leaning forward, mesmerized.

The autonomous bot's motor made him giddy and excited, but he kept his cool.

"Anna, what is this for?" Amelia asked. "Of what use is it to us?"

"This autonomous bot, as tiny as it is, detects diseases and ailments in seconds," Anna said. "When it discovers something, it will also provide top-notch professional advice and treatment options."

Amelia rolled her eyes in disbelief.

"My husband and I should lock you up for deceit and fraudulent acts, you know?"

"You and your husband *will* be locked up soon if you do not prove that your extreme measures were for the greater good," Anna said.

Amelia and Andrew stared back in disbelief, then looked at each other, dumbfounded.

But Anna kept going.

"Here is the remote control. You shall need to operate this." She dropped a tiny device on the table. "Keep it safe. Experiment with the controller. You never know when you will need it."

She clicked two buttons on the remote control and Amelia and Andrew stared with wide eyes as the autonomous bot returned to what it had been earlier—a simple metallic box. Without seeing it with their own eyes, no one could ever guess what it could become.

"We can still change Teleos, but that will only happen if you still believe in the power of your idea," Anna said.

"How did you get this?" Andrew asked, aiming to reach the box.

"Well, I have my ways. It is what you have always wanted, is it not?"

Andrew stared long and hard at the box. It felt unreal to him that after everything; he seemed to have got what he wanted, even when it felt like he had been cheated.

"When you need me, please find me before Master Theodore does. I need to go now," Anna said. "And don't forget; keep it safe."

With that, Anna headed for the door and left the office.

Amelia and Andrew stayed calm and still, staring back at the machine for a long stretch of time before someone spoke up.

"This does not seem good to me, Andrew," Amelia said. "We should return this. It doesn't seem right, and after the recent escapade, I think we should trust my instinct."

Andrew looked at Amelia and smiled gently. "Oh Amelia, just what if everything we experienced that night was just in our heads? I mean, Father said destruction awaits when we go into the building, but here is innovation. Life-changing innovation. Look at it.

"Besides, destruction did not come about, did it?"

"Andrew, you need to shake off that thought. We are in enough of a mess already. Can you not see that?"

"But what mess, exactly?" Andrew said. "Nothing has gone wrong since our experience. We have simply been overtaken by fear! I have to admit, it petrified me of what might happen."

Amelia stayed quiet, reasoning what Andrew had said.

It seemed true, almost as if they were punishing themselves, and that it wasn't too bad.

"The light in Abaddon went out after we went in," Andrew said, his eyes now wide with excitement. "What if we went there just to take the *blessings* that Father told us were *curses*?"

Amelia stayed quiet, hating there was some sense in what Andrew had said.

"We should not waste more time dying in guilt that is not even real!" Andrew said. He jumped to his feet and raised his clenched fist in the air. "I knew it felt right. It just did!"

"Since we got back, we have handled matters with ease and intelligence," Amelia added, after giving everything some thought. "Just like Father would."

Andrew nodded and walked to the window that overlooked the factory.

He placed both hands on the window stool and peered down at the workers.

"I will save all of Teleos," Andrew said. "One after the other, starting with Mr. Peter."

"Huh?" Amelia was not sure what he meant. "We are just back from the clinic, yes?"

"Yes," Andrew said, turning to face Amelia. "But now we have a solution to fully diagnose what is wrong with him, and the autonomous bot will also tell us how to treat him. I knew my idea would change the future of Teleos. We should lose no time in going back to see him."

Amelia smiled gently.

"That would be amazing, Andrew. To be able to detect what the doctors have not because of this machine. I sincerely apologize for not taking your idea as seriously as I should have."

"We are about to change Teleos, and Father should be so proud of us in what we have achieved without his input, but maybe—"

"What, Andrew?"

"I was going to say that maybe Father will be bitter because we have outdone him. Achieved something life-changing without his stamp of approval."

"We should go," Amelia said after they spent minutes looking at the machine in front of them. "We really should be on our way now. Perhaps we can help Mr. Peter and thus, please, Father."

They both agreed and headed out to the clinic. Phillip followed closely and Andrew refused his offer to help with the bag, his excitement increasing greatly on their way.

He knew how close he was to rewriting history in Teleos. He would be mentioned in centuries to come for what he was about to achieve and would allow nothing to get in the way. As they walked down the hallway, Andrew anticipated how well the autonomous bot would work.

"Sir!" a voice cried out. "Please, you can't be here!"

It was the same plump nurse they had met before.

"We have something that will help to diagnose," Andrew said confidently. "Tell the doctors I said so. This will change the future of medicine."

The nurse had a confused look, gazing at Andrew and Amelia from head to toe, and noticed the bag Andrew was holding. When she saw they were quite serious and unmoving, she started heading toward the doctor's office.

"If you could just wait here, I will go fetch a doctor."

Andrew found a free space in the waiting area, removed the box from the bag, and placed it on a chair. It looked very clean and sleek, and this gave him even more confidence. They waited patiently for the nurse to return, but instead, Michael met them.

"The nurse here says you want to see Mr. Peter?" Michael asked, walking toward Andrew from the doctor's office.

It shocked Andrew to see him.

"Michael," he managed to say. "It is a surprise to see you. Is my father here?"

"No, he is not, Andrew. Master has missed your presence in his quarters."

"Well, I and Amelia here have been busy tending to pressing issues in Teleos."

"That I can see," Michael said. "Would you like to come with me now? He is free and ready to receive you. I can assure you he's looking forward to seeing you both."

"Oh, um, I'm not too sure at the moment," Andrew said. He laughed uncomfortably and took a few steps backwards. "We were—"

"Andrew and I wish to sort a few more things before we see Father," Amelia said. "We would not like to put him in a state of worry or concern for Teleos."

"Yes, that's what I was about to say," Andrew said.

"That, I understand," Michael said. "Then I will pass this message to him when I return to the quarters. But please, you must be sure to visit him soon."

"Thank you, Michael," Andrew said.

"And, Andrew," Michael said as he was leaving. "You really should not be here. The sickness is spreading fast and the last thing Teleos needs is for you or Amelia to be taken down by it. Please take on board what the medical staff says. They are thinking about your well-being."

"Of course," Andrew said. "Come, Amelia. Michael is right about what he's saying."

He turned around, and they walked back to their workplace.

"So how do we do this?" Andrew asked when they both sat back in the mill.

"Maybe we should wait till tomorrow, and then we go in without permission."

"We should take some more time to know how this machine works, too," he said. "We need much practice in controlling it."

"Alright then," Amelia agreed.

They spent the remaining hours of the day within their four walls, doing all they could to get their mind off the guilt they were feeling for disobeying Father.

But even with the machine in their hands and the smell of success close by, the feeling of guilt was a tough stain that just would not go away.

Neither of them spoke about it, but it was in the air, in their movement, and in their silence.

Chapter 12: Aftermath

"**M**aster!" Michael charged into the room where Theodore sat. "Master, there is a big problem!"

As he entered the room in the late hours of the evening, he met Theodore standing in front of the window, staring straight ahead.

"What has happened in my city?" Theodore said in a weakened, deep tone.

Michael knew that tone.

Theodore had found out the greatest problem even before he could report it.

"Look," Theodore said, pointing out of the window to the ends of the city. "Where did the light go?"

"Master, Abaddon has prevailed over us!" Michael cried out. "No one saw who went in and out, but this explains the ruins that have been in the city for some days now."

"Ruins?"

"Unexplainable ruins, Master," Michael said. "The gold in Havilah no longer flows, an unknown sickness spreads in the factory and the clinic is having more patients than it can handle. The people are in complete confusion and rage."

"My city?" Theodore roared. "My city?"

"Master, it is all in the reports!" Michael cried out. "Unexplainable occurrences in the city, indescribable events. As people walk past Abaddon, the air they inhale causes them to gasp for air, their skins begin to itch and then boil, and they suddenly—"

"Enough!" Theodore shouted. He turned around and Michael saw his bloodshot eyes. "I have been betrayed!"

"M-master, who would dare betray you?" Michael asked, sensing Theodore's rage building, and he certainly didn't want to be on the receiving end of that.

Theodore charged into his chambers, summoning every man who worked directly for him—men who enforced his laws, the ones who kept the people in check, and the ones carrying out his commands. These were his most trusted.

Like a storm waiting to happen, these men appeared in the meeting hall in a short time, assembling before Theodore and Michael.

"Gentlemen, the day that we all have dreaded, that I have so dreaded and kept away from, has finally come," Theodore said. "The city of Teleos has stood tall over many years. It has stood tall not because of how powerful I am or how rich we are, or how resourceful our city is, but because of how united we have stood together, year after year, decade after decade."

The room remained silent, each man now understanding the severity of what Theodore was about to say. Most had never been summoned by their leader before.

"Decades ago, the city of ruins, Golgotha, tried to prevail from within the walls of Teleos. They built a house and dragged our people into it, destroying the bond these people had with Teleos and making them slaves against their wishes."

"Yes, Master," one man said. He was baldheaded and sounded enraged. "But with your leadership, we'll prevail."

"True," Theodore responded. "And I did all to teach my people to stay away from that building because the intent was clear."

Theodore stopped talking, walked to the window, turned around, and looked at the faces of the men standing before him. Phillip kneeled down before Theodore and cried out in a broken voice."Master, it was your son Andrew that went into Abaddon. No one said anything in response to this. They knew the law, and they knew their leader was just. "My own son has fallen for the trick of the enemy, and I must do what I must do to keep Teleos standing."Theodore gave no further explanation. He simply walked out of his quarters, the men following closely behind.

Feet rumbled in the hall as the men shifted from one foot to another, mumbling between themselves, expressing shock at what they had just heard.

"Silence!" Theodore said, turning around again. "My justice knows no name and will not be partial."

Michael tried to keep his cool.

This had not happened in years, not even in the last few decades.

The last time was during the war against the city of Golgotha when Theodore was highly provoked, and he commanded for the enemies to be ruined, which he achieved in minutes.

The men were in groups of tens, walking together but saying nothing.

Following Theodore's steps, they all stopped in front of the only other quarter in the same building—Andrew's residence.

"Andrew!" Theodore said.

He had not raised his voice, yet it thundered through the building.

There was no answer.

"Andrew!" Theodore said again. "Your filthy secret is out! Come out this instant!"

Michael stared in disbelief. Now it made sense.

Now he understood the reason why the city was slowly falling apart.

There was no other person in the whole of Teleos who would cause so much damage by visiting Abaddon except Theodore himself, or his offspring, Andrew.

The reports he had obtained from Teleos and the cities around were so different from what he would normally receive. Starting from the gold. It had never stopped flowing since the last war. It just kept flowing, so much that the golden mansion was built from the excess.

The sickness was unexplainable, and the medical team—revered by the whole of Teleos—failed to determine what the disease was. They were baffled.

The entire ambiance within the city was filled with pain and anger, and Michael could tell so easily. He feared there would be some kind of revolt from the people soon, as they were just not happy or living in peace.

From the insides of the quarters, Amelia, Anna and Andrew stood terrified in the study.

They had heard the heavy knock on the door but tried to ignore it.

"Oh, I should not have come here tonight," Anna cried out.

She sat on a chair, remote in hand and machine on her lap. Andrew had invited her over so they could master the use of the machine with her guidance.

"Andrew! Come out here this instant," Theodore said. "You have failed me, and you have failed your city."

Dropping to the ground, Andrew buried his face in his hands, attempting to hide from his father's rage. Amelia was in a state of confusion. Some minutes ago, they had been so sure that all was going well and there would be no repercussions for what they had done.

They had been making plans for the autonomous bot to diagnose the patients.

Now, it had all blown up in their faces, with Master Theodore right outside their quarters.

After minutes of silence from all three, Andrew finally stood up.

"Let us go," Andrew said. "Father knows all, and we must come clean. Enough of the hiding."

Anna cried out. "We will be doomed!"

Andrew shot her a bitter glance. "Do you have a better option? You should have thought of your doom when you deceived my wife and me into that hellhole you called an eating house."

Andrew took Amelia's hands as she was sobbing uncontrollably.

"Let us go," he said. "Father will forgive us, but not this witch. We need to face his wrath."

He helped her up, and soon they appeared before Theodore and the rest of his men.

"You have done that I said you must not do," Theodore said when they opened the door. "Is there anything you lacked that you did not receive?"

"No, Father," Andrew said, looking to the ground. He had seen the many men standing outside of the quarters and with this, even he knew that mercy was not possible.

"Did I withhold anything at all from you?"

"No, Father."

"Did you for once feel neglected, as if I was unfair to you?"

"No, Father," Andrew said again.

"Then why did you choose to destroy the city that I trusted you with? Why did you go after what I said was destruction and disdain? How many times did I tell you to never go near the house with the bright lights, or even to talk about it?"

"They tricked us, Father," Amelia cried out. "She tricked us! She lied to us, told us she was our friend, and led us straight to doom."

"And who is it that you speak of?" Theodore asked.

"Anna," Amelia said, pointing into the house where Anna was. "Come out, you deceiver!"

Anna came out and Theodore looked sternly at her, even if she could not maintain eye contact.

"You!" Theodore said. "Morana, daughter of Golgotha."

"What—" Amelia gasped. She had only heard of Golgotha from her parents when she was much younger, but she had never expected this to happen.

"Quiet!" Theodore cut Amelia off. "You, Andrew, have sold your right to be called a leader in this city. I had no doubt I could trust you and steer you to become a great leader. But you have failed me and, more importantly, you have failed the people of Teleos."

"Father, I did it all for Teleos! I did it so Teleos could grow and rank even higher than it already is," Andrew found the courage to say. "Look at the city of gold! It has helped place us in a position we have never been in. We now have visitors traveling from afar to see our city, paying to see, paying to sleep, and paying to eat here! I wanted more for us!"

Theodore shook his head when he heard this.

"You mean the gold that stands in a vast lump you dare to call a mansion? That great lump that leaves us penniless when we need to donate to the poor or go on a trade mission? What are we to do, Andrew—are we to say to the farmer that he may come to kiss the great mansion in exchange for a pig? Are we to tell the starving man with his emaciated children he should come and behold the glory that is our shining golden palace... if he can crawl there?"

"Father, give us a chance, please! We have failed you and we are sorry. But Teleos can stand tall beside all the cities in the region and even beyond. I merely wished to be the same kind of progressive man, a man of technology, as you have been. I wanted only to please you!"

"You try to please me by lying, cheating, disobedience, flouting the rules, by being arrogant, pigheaded, stubborn, a know-it-all, and egotistical! Well, how did that turn out for you, Andrew ."

Andrew looked around himself and tried to crawl inside of the house.

Every pair of eyes focused on him with a look of rage and disgust.

"Do not move, Andrew," Theodore said. "You have no right to."

"Father, please let me show you what we have done for Teleos," Andrew said. "See, the first of its kind in the entire region. We have built a autonomous bot that will help diagnose diseases, Father!"

"Oh, Andrew! Are you now blind?"

"Father, please believe me. I beg you. This autonomous bot will change Teleos for good and will make diseases so much easier to tackle. Look, Mr. Peter has been in isolation and under close watch for days. Now, more people have joined him, and no one knows why yet. What if we diagnose this and find a way out earlier?"

By this time, Andrew did not care that other people were right there, hearing everything.

He just needed a way out of his father's wrath.

"Those people are only falling deathly sick because of your disobedience," Theodore said. "The disease is spreading because you neglected my instructions and you went your own way, the way you thought was best. You have brought a scourge, a plague, upon our city."

"But, Father," Andrew said.

"I will not hear it! You have been misled because of your quest for power and the greed that you allowed to fill your heart. The machine you think you have is a tool for even more destruction and is cursed by your hands for touching it."

The entire place was filled with silence for some seconds, and with deep pain in his eyes, Theodore looked away. He did not want to punish them, but he had to.

Amelia was ashamed to have become embroiled in this hideous mess and was mortified to have said nothing to Theodore, despite her promises to warn him if Andrew went astray.

Anna couldn't face him or the great number of men standing before her.

She, too, wondered how everything had happened so fast and how the lady she had met in Abaddon successfully turned her against her good friend.

Theodore sighed deeply and looked at all three of them on their knees.

"I am a just leader, and I will not let evil go unpunished," Theodore said, his voice trembling a little, but he carried on. "If only you had come to me when things had gone south, there would have been a way out. You failed to see that only I could help you out of a mess."

"All three of you have opened your hearts even more for the enemy to rule."

Amelia's heart broke when she heard this.

She could not take the burning pain she felt in her chest, and she clung to it for dear life.

"If I spare you, then my city will crumble before my very eyes and my people will no longer have trust in me. Do you know how long it takes for one to gain trust? To have this respect and understanding amongst such noble people?"

"Father, please forgive us!"

"Oh no, Son. You all have been forgiven, even long before you asked. But you must bear the consequence of your disobedience, or I will not be the just leader that I claim to be."

"But you are not the leader, Father. I am," pleaded the voice of Andrew in a pathetic whine.

Theodore signaled to a group of men directly behind, and they moved in.

They roughly took hold of Andrew, Amelia, and Anna.

"Because you have disobeyed me and brought harm to the city of Teleos and its people, you have now stripped yourselves of the right to remain here in this city. You are no longer the leader, Andrew.

"This life of ease and plenty you have forfeited, and you will be sent out from here, far from us, to start life all by yourself. You must not be seen, ever again, with any of the citizens of the city of Teleos. Neither will you benefit from any of its resources."

"Father, please forgive us," Amelia cried.

She had been sobbing quietly but was now hit by the weight of this punishment.

"The pain I feel in my heart as my son- and daughter-in-law disobeyed me, you both will also feel as you begin to have your own children," Theodore said bitterly.

One man stood beside him, taking notes.

"And you, Morana," Theodore said. "You chose to deceive my son and his chosen wife, persuading them to turn their backs on me."

"No, Master. Amelia and I had a good childhood together. When I returned to Teleos, a spirit that I did not know about, Master possessed me," Anna said. "It controlled me and made me do things I did not know."

"You should not have gone there," Theodore said. "If you did not have bitterness, greed, and jealousy in your heart, the enemy would have found nowhere to fix its claws.

"As for you, may you continue to toil all the rest of your life and be far away from this city. You think that you have seen hardship, but I will ensure that you are rejected from the entire region. I will not kill you, but I will place a price on your head throughout the land.

"Anyone who sees you will take it upon themselves, in allegiance to their leader, to bring your head to me."

Michael shook his head in disbelief.

He was in shock, and he was sad as well. The effect of their offense had not eaten deep into the city yet, but it certainly would have if Theodore had not instructed him to go around the entire city and try to find out more of the goings on.

"And you, Phillip," Theodore said. "I gave you charge to be my son's protector, and you allowed this to happen."

"Master, I only followed orders! Please, have mercy on me."

"If I do, you will corrupt the rest of my people who are loyal to me," Theodore said. "For this, you will forever remain the servant to my son and his wife. Where they go, you must go too. You must protect their lives at all costs and do all that is asked of you to do."

Another of Theodore's men walked forward and took Phillip by the hand, leading him away.

"I have spoken." Theodore turned around and walked away without looking back.

The cries from Amelia and Anna echoed in the hallway, piercing through the night.

Andrew and Amelia walked out through the gate of the city for the first time in a long time, with Anna and Phillip close behind. They were not allowed to take anything with them, not even their clothes or things from their own quarters. They walked fast with their heads bowed.

"I should have focused on helping Teleos manage with what it already had," Andrew said bitterly as they walked. It was a walk of shame, as the entire city knew what had happened. Theodore had sent out word that no one must accommodate them in Teleos and even in the surrounding cities.

Passing through the gateway, they saw the building of their downfall again.

"How could we be so blind to this? To the one thing that we had been warned about repeatedly? Why was I so stupid?"

Amelia had not said a word since they left the quarters. Her heart was shattered, and she would occasionally place her hand over her chest, trying to manage the pain.

"How did we allow the enemy to creep in on us so quietly, and we never suspected or noticed that we were entering into our own doom?"

Andrew looked back at the city, remembering how smooth and painless life was when he was under the watch and guidance of his father. He remembered how happy he felt when he pleased his father, and how easily he carried out his will to help Teleos grow even more.

Now, everything flashed before his eyes, and it was all gone.

"Greed," Amelia finally said. "We wanted more, we wanted it all."

"But we had everything," Andrew said. "What more did we need?"

"The enemy made us think we were missing out on something, and we crawled right into their trap. People would have died for just half of what we had, Andrew. But no, we wanted more."

They kept walking, each step taking them farther away from their paradise.

"Anna," Amelia called out. "Why did you do this?"

"The enemy used me to reach you," Anna cried out, dragging her feet as she went. "I was jealous of you and everything you had. The enemy built on that and made me his puppet."

Amelia shook her head in disbelief and the gate was shut as soon as Phillip passed through

Reality dawned on Andrew again and he fell to his knees, regretting his disobedience.

He looked at Abaddon and saw how wretched it really was.

But more than that—he looked at himself, seeing how he was even more wretched because if he had not been avaricious, if he just hadn't sought for fame, glory and pride, he would never have fallen for that dirty trick that led him astray, but no. He had been jealous of his own Father, wanting to shine in technology just like his father did.

Yet he had failed to realize how long it had taken his father to know how far to go. He had failed to respect the years of dedication and toil his father had invested, assuming it would all come to him because he wanted it, rather than because he deserved it.

"That light was the one thing that called us in," Anna said. "It appeared like the best thing in all of Teleos."

"I had the best thing," Andrew said. "I had fellowship with my father, and it made me wise. It was only when I strayed from my father that I grew unwise, inviting evil in."

Amelia was still quiet as they walked farther into the unknown.

"Abaddon had nothing to offer. Nothing but confusion and a chase for greed," Andrew said. "Oh, how stupid I was to throw my life away and pick death. Throw gold away and pick stones."

Phillip wept bitterly in his heart. He regretted staying silent about all that had happened.

It was getting dark, and they had been walking for some time, so they decided it was best to cut their journey in half. Surely, they were far enough away from Teleos that no one would recognize who they were and what they had done.

"I really think we should try to rest for the night. Make a fresh start tomorrow," Phillip said. "I will approach the next person we come across to see if they will put us up for the night."

"Good idea, Phillip," Andrew said. "There's a woman right over there, look."

"Hello, madam," Phillip called out to the woman standing outside her house. "If it's not too much trouble, could we please take shelter in your home for the night? We would be on our way at the break of dawn."

"And why would I agree to that? Word travels fast, you know," the woman said. "You must consider yourself blessed that Master did not order your deaths," the woman called out. "You have no idea of the havoc you caused by unleashing the darkness of Abaddon."

"But we have learned a valuable lesson. We would not be any trouble, I promise you that," Andrew jumped in. "I will make sure of it. I give you my word."

"I know you won't be any trouble, but I will not agree to let you in. Do you take everyone for gullible fools?"

"Your word means nothing to anyone anymore. You really don't know the damage you have caused. You have managed to destroy so much in such a little amount of time. You must leave now, or I will inform the Master of this. And he will come over and pick up the meat cleaver we keep by the door and chop off your head."

She said nothing more and walked towards her home. "Oh, and don't be surprised if you get the same response from the next person you approach with your foolish, self-centered suggestions. Now, please leave, and never come back!"

She banged the door shut behind herself.

Chapter 13:
Pandora's Box

The festival had finally arrived, and by this time, Teleos was back in perfect shape. Theodore had rallied his men and worked twice as hard to ensure the city was back to its former glory.

Theodore took time off to replay everything in his head.

He had sent away his only son for his wrongs and he was left all alone again, but he had no alternative and was sure they would be safe.

All he knew was they needed to be punished for their offense and could no longer stay within the walls of Teleos; the enemy had eaten into their hearts and planted greed, rebellion, and disobedience, things that weren't accepted in his city.

With his mind now focused on the daily running of the city, Theodore soon overcame his emotions, his presence reassuring his people.

The general feeling of positivity and prosperity had now been restored.

"Master," Michael said, entering the quarters. "We started clearing out Andrew's quarters today and we found this."

Michael handed the metal box and remote he had found to Theodore.

"Oh dear. The enemy really did try to creep in on us while we slept," Theodore said. "Do you know what this is, Michael?"

"N-no Master," Michael replied. "No, I do not."

"It is Pandora's box," he said. "The very one that comes from Golgotha."

Michael looked confused, still unsure what it was for.

"Michael, if this box had been opened by anyone in Teleos, the city would have become home to demons and evil. There would be no stopping it. Whatever would come would have taken over the whole city and spread beyond."

Michael stared in disbelief.

"Master. I saw Andrew holding that same box when I saw him in the clinic the other day," he said. "He was asking to be allowed to Mr. Peter's ward, but I advised him to stay away as the disease was spreading. What if I hadn't been there? I dread to think what would have happened."

Theodore sighed and shook his head.

"Michael, it was a godsend that you were there and acted the way you did. These are trying times, hard times, and we must stay vigilant," he said. "The enemy saw an opportunity to use Andrew's authority within the city in exchange for a filthy box that Andrew thought was the way forward in Teleos. What a waste."

Theodore stared at the box for a few more minutes, then asked Michael to take it away.

"Michael, as I have explained, this box must not be opened. It should be destroyed completely in an enclosed space and make sure you watch it burn till the very end."

"Okay, Master," Michael said. "I will do just that. We have already had one lucky escape."

The miniature autonomous bot was taken to the extreme of the city where it was destroyed, and the rest of the quarters were checked and cleaned out.

The following day, Theodore accompanied Michael on an inspection of the quarters and the building as a whole. "What more is there to do?" Theodore said.

"The festival is fast approaching, and plans are still being made toward it. We have summoned doctors from all over the region, playing their part in the collective effort to treat the fast-spreading sickness. Their strategy seems to work fine."

"And the factory?"

"Still up and running, Master," Michael said. "The workers are a lot calmer, and well taken care of."

"Is there still panic among the leaders that are due to visit soon? I hear they fear the presence of the sickness in Teleos, and a good number were reluctant to attend the festival."

"Not anymore, Sir. In fact, they started arriving last night, and we have received no cancellations. So, all in all, Sir, things are progressing nicely."

Theodore was pleased. Havilah's gold production was thriving once again and things were running seamlessly with no concerns whatsoever. It was reported that the gold reserves had been attacked and the workers present there at the time were abducted, bound, gagged, and locked away in a room under the building. Their families had gone searching for them, spreading fear in the city, adding on to the tense situation.

But all of that was now over, and things had been restored.

Theodore wished more than anything that he could get his children back to experience the glory that they would be missing out on, but it was the price he had to pay for purity and order in Teleos, and he did not regret one bit of it.

The days following the departure of Andrew and Amelia were filled with celebration and fun.

When those from the neighboring cities came to celebrate, Teleos was just as they had known it to be—the most remarkable city for miles around.

This year was no different, with Theodore addressing the leaders from the numerous cities.

"The city is on a firm and solid foundation," Theodore announced to the leaders at the beginning of the festival. "We will not be shaken and whoever invites harm or evil will be picked up and thrown out before they infect the others. If I can ask you all to pass this on through your communities when you return home. As you are aware, regardless of whoever tries to ruin this great city, they will be dealt with in the same nature. There will be no favoritism or forgiveness, and the punishment shall be the same for each," Theodore added. "Thank you for your time and please enjoy the festival."

The ceremony was filled with laughter, and the joy of the people made the entire city lively again. The air in Teleos felt clean, and it was now a lot easier to breathe.

Everything was magnificent—well, almost everything.

"What is that at the gate?" the leader of Ashur said to Theodore when they had just finished breakfast. "You know, the young children asked me to describe your magnificent city before we arrived and when they saw this missing detail, they tugged at me for not adding it to the story."

Theodore laughed loudly and walked to the window in his dining hall to see what his good friend was talking about. Right at the gate of the city where Abaddon once stood was a huge fire, seemingly having no beginning and no end, and visible for as far as the eye could see.

"That, my friend," Theodore said, "is a reminder to the ones who went against my wishes—the rejected ones—to stay as far away from Teleos for as long as possible."

"Rejected ones?"

"Yes. The ones who are now enemies of the city, the ones who bring pain and destruction, and the ones who wish to overthrow me."

"Hmm. That is very much needed, Theodore," the leader said. "It should also serve as a reminder to the ones within Teleos, warning them of the price that can and will be paid for enmity. I am so relieved to have you back. Someone who knows the true meaning of how one should present themselves to others. And you always were our most remarkable leader."

"Thank you, and you are right," Theodore said. "If my own son who sat at *my* table to eat with me and knew the issues of Teleos more than anyone else in the entire city could fall for the trick of the enemy, then anyone else can be fooled too! I told him so many times about the repercussions if anyone were to enter Abaddon, and he still went ahead against my strict instructions. What more could I have done than warn them of the consequences?"

"You did the right thing, Theodore—everybody knows and appreciates that. In their greed for the new, they forgot the ways of the old and they have paid a mighty price for that."

Theodore called the fire by the gates 'the flaming sword' and it was now the brightest light in the city, replacing the previous one of Abaddon tenfold. It was visible from miles around.

Trudging on hopelessly, to nowhere in particular, Andrew and Amelia saw it from afar and no matter how far away they went, they would no doubt keep seeing it, reminding them of the deceit toward Andrew's father and the whole city of Teleos. They understood it was there to keep them away, and to remind them of how irresponsible they had been.

They had completely sabotaged their place in the city of Teleos.

Standing and looking back toward the immense fire, Andrew placed a hand on Amelia's shoulder.

"Why did I do it? Why couldn't I accept what I already had—which was far more than anyone would ever need—and listen to Father? Why, Amelia? Why?"

Amelia said nothing, peering at the fire in the distance, a tear running down her cheek.

What she wanted to say was, *"why didn't you listen to me either?"*

Please continue to support this author. This is the first series of stories inspired by the Bible.

Please visit www.keeponkeepingonpc.com